Nelly the
MONSTER
Sitter

To the Fentons at number three

First published in Great Britain in 2005
by Hodder Children's Books

2 4 6 8 10 9 7 5 3 1

A Catalogue record for this book is available
from the British Library

ISBN 0 340 88433 9

Typeset in Baskerville by Avon DataSet Ltd,
Bidford-on-Avon, Warwickshire

Printed and bound in Great Britain by
Bookmarque Ltd, Croydon, Surrey

The paper and board used in this paperback by Hodder Children's Books are natural recyclable products made from wood grown in sustainable forests. The manufacturing processes conform to the environmental regulations of the country of origin.

Hodder Children's Books
A division of Hodder Headline Ltd
338 Euston Road
London NW1 3BH

Nelly the MONSTER Sitter

Cowcumbers, Pipplewaks & Altigators

KES GRAY

Illustrated by Stephen Hanson

A division of Hodder Headline Limited

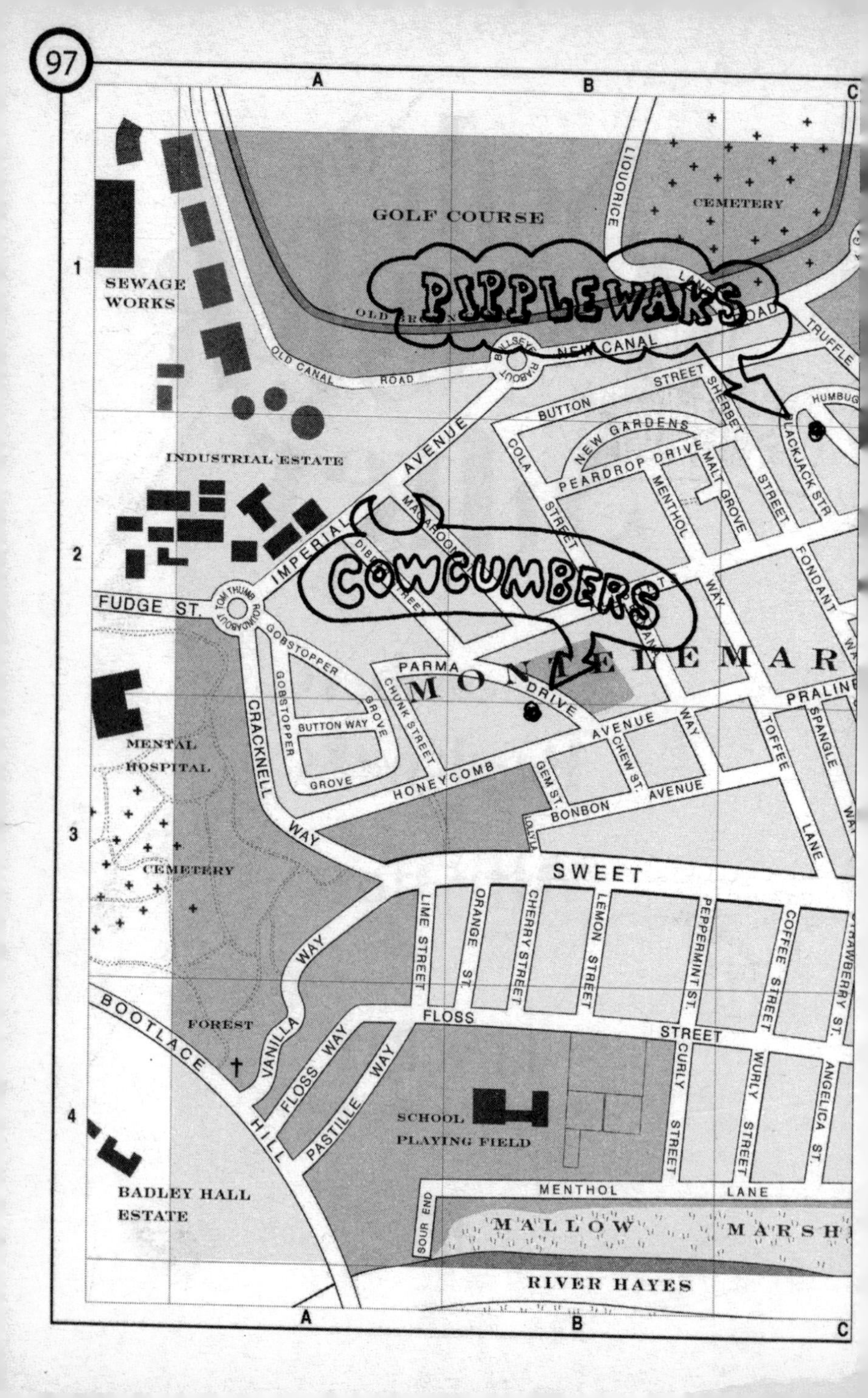

97
A
B
C
1
2
3
4
GOLF COURSE
CEMETERY
LIQUORICE
PIPPLEWAKS
OLD CANAL ROAD
NEW CANAL
TRUFFLE
SEWAGE WORKS
INDUSTRIAL ESTATE
STREET
SHERBET
HUMBUG
BUTTON
NEW GARDENS
COLA
PEARDROP DRIVE
MALT
MENTHOL
GROVE
STREET
BLACKJACK STR
AVENUE
IMPERIAL
COWCUMBERS
FONDANT
WAY
FUDGE ST.
TOM THUMB ROUNDABOUT
GOBSTOPPER
PARMA
DRIVE
PRALINE
CHUNK STREET
GROVE
BUTTON WAY
GOBSTOPPER
GROVE
CRACKNELL
MENTAL HOSPITAL
AVENUE
WAY
CHEW ST.
TOFFEE
SPANGLE
HONEYCOMB
GEM ST.
BONBON
AVENUE
LANE
WAY
CEMETERY
SWEET
LIME STREET
ORANGE ST.
CHERRY STREET
LEMON STREET
PEPPERMINT ST.
COFFEE STREET
VANILLA WAY
BOOTLACE
FOREST
FLOSS
STREET
FLOSS WAY
PASTILLE WAY
HILL
CURLY STREET
WURLY STREET
ANGELICA ST.
SCHOOL
PLAYING FIELD
BADLEY HALL ESTATE
MENTHOL
LANE
SOUR END
MALLOW
RIVER HAYES
A
B
C

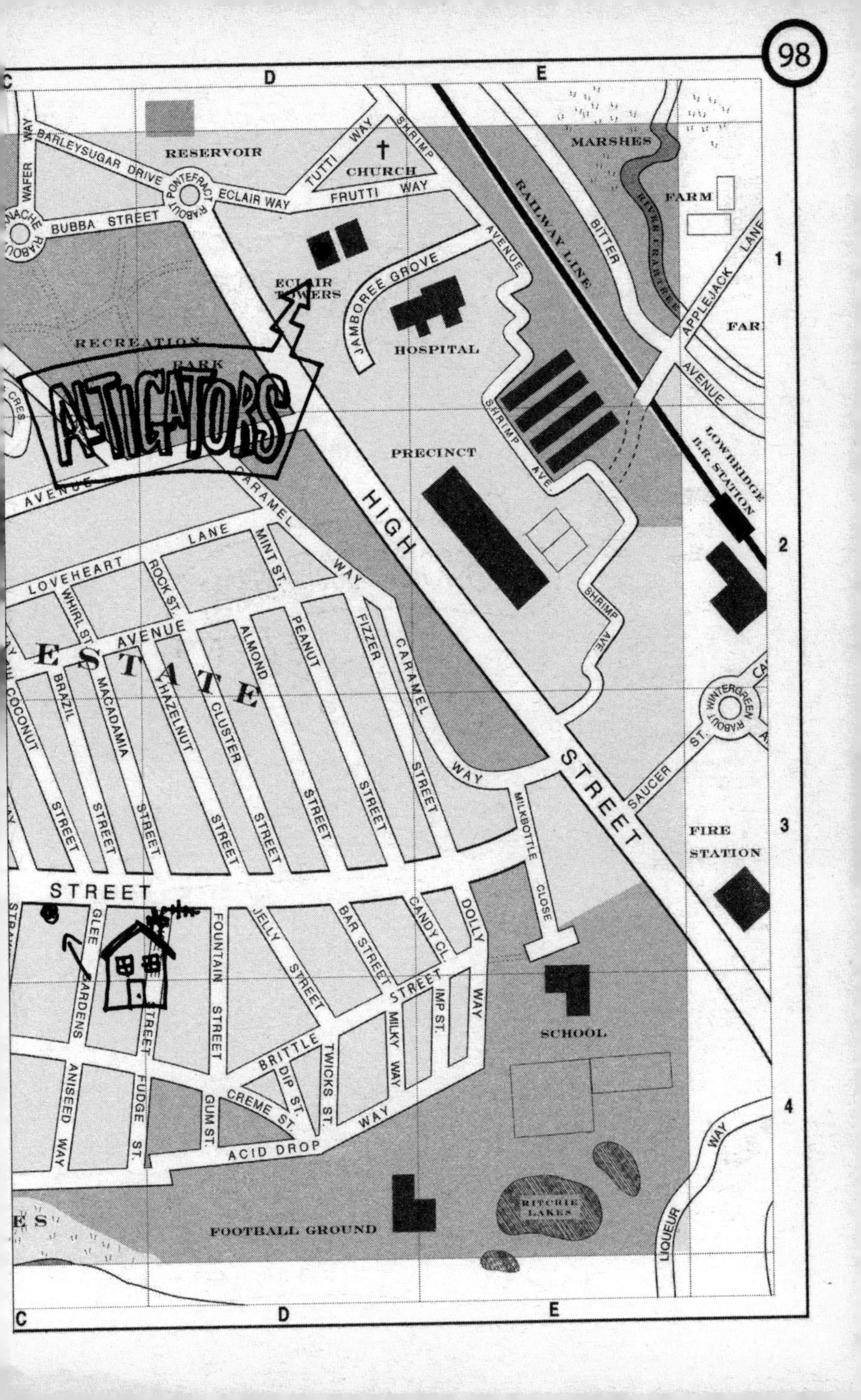
C
D
E
1
2
3
4
RESERVOIR
WAFER WAY
BARLEYSUGAR DRIVE
PONTEFRACT RABOUT
ECLAIR WAY
BUBBA STREET
TUTTI WAY
SHRIMP
CHURCH
FRUTTI WAY
MARSHES
RAILWAY LINE
BITTER
RIVER CRABTREE
FARM
APPLEJACK LANE
AVENUE
ECLAIR TOWERS
JAMBOREE GROVE
HOSPITAL
RECREATION PARK
ALLIGATORS
SHRIMP AVE.
PRECINCT
LOWBRIDGE B.R. STATION
AVENUE
CARAMEL WAY
HIGH STREET
LANE
MINT ST.
LOVEHEART AVENUE
ROCK ST.
WHIRL ST
ESTATE
COCONUT STREET
BRAZIL STREET
MACADAMIA STREET
HAZELNUT STREET
CLUSTER STREET
ALMOND STREET
PEANUT STREET
FIZZER STREET
CARAMEL STREET
WINTERGREEN RABOUT
SAUCER ST.
FIRE STATION
MILKBOTTLE CLOSE
STREET
GLEE GARDENS
FOUNTAIN STREET
JELLY STREET
BAR STREET
CANDY CL.
DOLLY WAY
IMP ST.
MILKY WAY
BRITTLE STREET
DIP ST.
TWICKS ST.
CREME ST.
WAY
SCHOOL
ANISEED WAY
FUDGE ST.
GUM ST.
ACID DROP
FOOTBALL GROUND
RITCHIE LAKES
LIQUEUR WAY
C
D
E

NELLY THE MONSTER SITTER

'If monsters are real, how come I've never seen one?' said Nelly.

'Because they never go out,' said her dad.

'Why don't monsters ever go out?' said Nelly.

'Because they can never get a baby sitter,' said her dad.

Nelly thought about it. Her mum and dad never went out unless they could get a baby sitter. Why should monsters be any different?

'Then I shall become Nelly the Monster Sitter!' smiled Nelly.

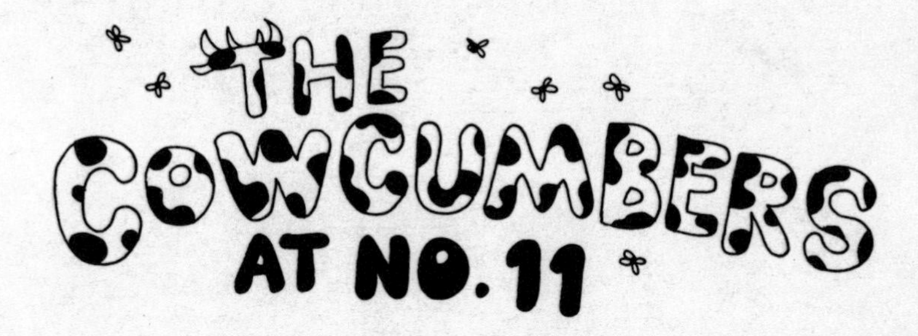
THE
COWCUMBERS
AT NO. 11

1

The telly in Nelly's house had blown up, halfway through an episode of *Summerdale Farm*. One minute Dilys Burton from the post office was about to pack her bags and run away to Spain with Bernie Melrose from the farm, the next minute the telly had gone bang, the screen had gone blank and Dilys and Bernie had vanished, ahead of schedule.

For one frenzied moment everyone in the Morton family had become an expert on TV repairs. Nelly's dad had whacked it, Mum had kicked it, Nelly had shaken it and Asti had glared at it. But nothing had worked. The telly was totally kaput.

'Typical,' groaned Asti. 'Just when we were getting to the juicy bit, too.'

'I reckon Dilys's husband intercepts them at the airport,' said Dad.

'I reckon Bernie forgets his passport and they have to go back for it and Jason is waiting for them,' said Nelly's mum.

'I reckon Bernie has a heart attack at the wheel, but his sheepdog saves the day by giving him the kiss of life and driving them to the airport. Halfway down the motorway, Dilys realises it isn't Bernie she really loves, it's Patch the sheepdog and so after a quick kiss and cuddle they dump Bernie in the car park at a motorway service station and run away to Spain together where they open a flamenco bar and live happily ever after.'

Everyone turned and looked at Nelly.

'Only kidding,' smiled Nelly.

'It's an interesting theory, though,' chuckled her dad. 'I'd like to see a sheepdog become a flamenco-dancing instructor.'

'Olé!' said Nelly's mum, leaping from the armchair and clicking her heels on the carpet.

'Dogs can't dance,' said Asti, who hadn't quite managed to enter into the spirit of the conversation, 'or drive taxis.'

'You're right,' said Nelly's mum, plonking herself back into her chair. 'What are we going to do now?'

Everyone stared blankly at the TV screen.

'We'll do what everyone used to do before telly was invented!' declared Dad.

'What was that, then?' asked Mum.

Dad opened his mouth, closed it slowly and then stared blankly back at the screen.

'People probably polished their dinosaurs,' said Nelly.

'Dinosaurs are too big to polish,' countered Asti.

'I'll tell you what people used to do before tellies were invented,' said Mum. 'They used to tidy their bedrooms!'

Nelly and Asti dispelled that theory immediately with acid-etched stares.

'We could play cards,' said Dad.

'We haven't got any cards,' said Mum. 'Auntie Vi was sick on them last Christmas.'

Nelly and Asti shuddered at the memory of Auntie Vi face-down on the table after drinking three too many sherry cocktails.

'How about charades?' said Dad. 'We enjoyed playing charades last Christmas!'

'*You* enjoyed playing charades last Christmas, Clifford. No one else did,' said Mum.

'Come on, Nelly, you go first!' said Dad, who had suddenly become brimful of Christmas spirit, despite it being the middle of June.

'Do I have to?' sighed Nelly, trying to hide behind a newspaper.

'It's more fun than tidying your room,' said Dad, who was now perched on the edge of his armchair, ready to play.

Nelly eased herself weakly out of her chair and stood limply in front of her family.

'What is it? Is it a film? Is it a play? Is it a book? Is it a song?' asked her dad, eagerly.

Nelly stood bolt upright. 'It's a phone call!' she

said, running out of the lounge and racing up the stairs. She had been saved by the bell – the distinctive trilling ring of the telephone in her bedroom.

'Must dash! Someone needs me to monster sit!' she shouted back to them. 'Asti can take my go!'

Asti groaned and buried her face in some cushions as Nelly flew into her bedroom and picked up the phone.

'Hello!' she panted. 'Nelly the Monster Sitter here!'

'Hello, it's Bello!' mooed a deep, resonating voice at the other end. 'I was wondering if yooooou could possibly monster sit for us toooooonight from six-thirty tooooo nine-thirty.'

It was the Cowcumbers from Number 11 Parma Drive.

'I would love to, Bello old fellow!' said Nelly, unable to resist the rhyme. 'How's Teet and Petal? Would they like me to bring anything?'

There was a slight pause followed by a 'Yoooooooooou could bring a long piece of rope if you like . . . Petal has a wobbly toooooooooth!'

Nelly gave her own teeth a quick once-over with her tongue. She always found it difficult to 'talk teeth' without wiggling her tongue round her own gnashers.

'I think you should let nature take its course!' she laughed, wondering whether or not monsters ever went to the dentist.

'We'll see yoooooooou at six-thirty, Nelly,' mooed Bello.

'Yoooooou certainly will!' laughed Nelly.

Nelly had monster sat for the Cowcumbers before. She had been recommended to them in the Easter holidays by her Huffaluk friends, Grit and Blob. That was the good thing about monster sitting: once word had got round, every monster in the neighbourhood had wanted to meet her.

Nelly hid in her bedroom for the next two hours, careful not to return downstairs until the very last minute possible, for fear of being dragged into the dreaded game of charades. When she walked into the lounge things were just as she had suspected. Her dad was still going strong, hogging centre stage and waving his arms around like a Shakespearean actor. Asti and her mum, on the other hand, were crushed with boredom and trying desperately to lose themselves like small change down the back of the settee.

'Help them out, Nelly,' said her dad, grateful for some fresh input. 'It's a book. Ten words. The fourth word is *the* and the seventh word sounds like *Himalayas*.'

Nelly looked towards the settee. It was one of those rare moments in life when she actually felt sorry for her sister.

'Sorry, Dad, I've got to go out,' she said. 'I'm monster sitting for the Cowcumbers. I'll leave their number on the mirror again.'

'Can I come?' mouthed her mum in silent desperation.

Nelly smiled and shook her head. Even Asti looked keener to monster sit than play charades with Dad.

Nelly mouthed a 'Sorry' back at her mum and then skipped towards the front door. 'I'll see you later,' she said. 'I'll be back around nine-thirty. Have fun!'

As Nelly stepped out into the evening sunshine, Nelly's mum sprung out of her seat and curtailed her husband's theatrics with a new charade of her own. It was an order. Six words. One exclamation mark . . . *Ring the Telly Repair Man Now!*

* * *

Nelly walked along Sweet Street, fondly recalling the moment when she had knocked on the Cowcumbers' door for the first time. Asti had teased her remorselessly that day, predicting that a Cowcumber would be half cucumber, and suggesting that Nelly might want to take some salad cream.

Nelly had slammed the front door furiously in Asti's face before leaving and by the time she had reached the door of Number 11 Parma Drive, had managed, out of principle, to avoid forming any preconceived ideas of how a Cowcumber might appear.

To her annoyance, Asti hadn't been entirely wrong. When the cream-coloured door of Number 11 had opened, all Nelly had been able to do was look upwards and nod.

Both Cowcumber parents had stood on two hooved legs and towered almost three metres high above the doormat. Their bodies were cucumber green and cucumber shaped, but their smooth, leathery skin had the black splodgy markings of a Freesian dairy cow.

Bello, the father, had two warm, toffee-coloured eyes nestling above a wet and glistening punchball of a nose. His head was large and as smooth as a bowling ball, and it was crowned with five yellow horns.

His wife Teet's facial features were marginally more feminine. Her eyes were red, her nose glistened orange and although her head was similarly ten-pin in shape, it was covered in salmon-pink dingle dangles. At first glance Nelly had thought they were hair curlers, but as Teet had curtsied lower to greet Nelly it had become clear that they were in fact udders! Teet had udders on her head! They were soft and curler length, with the flip-floppy wobble of small dreadlocks.

Nelly took time out from her recollections to cross Sweet Street. With a hop and a smile she leapt the kerb on the other side and cut diagonally through in the direction of Parma Drive.

It was a beautiful summer evening. Clouds of midges danced beside the hawthorn hedges that lined the footpath and every blackbird in the vicinity seemed to be in full chirrup. Nelly breathed deeply as she passed the sickly sweet

whiff of a pile of freshly-mown grass cuttings.

When the footpath petered out, Nelly took a right into the shadier environs of Bonbon Avenue and then a sharp left into Gem Street.

I hope Petal's cold has cleared up, she thought, remembering the size of the sticky sneeze that she had had to shovel off the wallpaper last time she had monster sat for the Cowcumbers.

She checked her pockets for tissues. 'I REALLY DO hope Petal's cold has cleared up!' she muttered, coming up empty-handed.

Tissues or no tissues, she was about to find out. She stepped into Honeycomb Avenue, turned into Parma Drive and skipped across the road. She was just two doors away from Number 11 now.

The Cowcumbers liked cream. Not only was their front door cream, but their window frames were painted cream, their front step was white-washed cream, even the roses that lined the front path were cream.

If you liked cream, this was the house for you.

Nelly trotted up the path, smoothed the

wrinkles from her sweatshirt and reached for the doorbell. It tinkled softly like a cowbell.

Cream porch-light, too, she thought, staring up at the spiders' webs that had been woven around the light bulb.

The front door swung open and two small black hooves threw themselves around Nelly's knees. It was Petal.

'Hello, Nelly, good to see yoooooooou again!' she mooed.

Nelly looked down at a wobble of yellow and blue udders. 'Hello tooooooo yoooooou tooooooo! I hear you've got a wobbly tooth!' she laughed, giving the top of Petal's head an affectionate ruffle.

Petal was too excited to talk teeth. She gave her wobbly tooth a wiggle with her tongue and then yanked Nelly into the hall.

'Come and see what we've got!' she mooed, releasing Nelly's knees and clip-clopping down the cream-tiled floor of a cream-wallpapered hallway. 'Come and see, Nelly, it's brand neeeeeewwwwwwww!'

'Hello Nelly, good to see yoooooou again!'

Nelly caught her breath. What an exciting welcome! She wiped her feet on the cream doormat, closed the front door and followed Petal into the lounge.

There she found Teet and Bello standing with their cucumber-green backs to her, staring intently at the far wall.

'What dooooo yoooooou think, Nelly?' mooed Petal, running beneath her mum's legs and jumping up and down excitedly in front of a giant black plasma screen which stretched from one side of the lounge wall to the other.

Teet and Bello turned and greeted Nelly with warm cloven hugs.

'Hello! Lovely tooooo see yooouu again, Nelly. How have yoooou been?'

Nelly waited for them to de-hug before attempting to speak.

'I'm very well thank yoooou,' she gasped. 'It's lovely to be back.'

'Well, we know what yoooooou twoooooooo will be doooing this evening!' mooed Bello, turning back to the screen and jabbing at it with the remote control.

The black plasma sprang to life, turning every colour of the spectrum before flicking randomly to Channel 43.

'Cool!' said Nelly. 'You've got widescreen!'

'It's not widescreen, Nelly, it's Weirdscreen,' mooed Petal.

'It's the very latest model, Nelly,' boasted Bello.

'We only got it today!' mooed Petal excitedly.

'Much better than widescreen,' wobbled Teet.

'Shame it isn't cream,' smiled Nelly mischievously.

'Doooooo yoooooou know, we were thinking exactly the same thing, Nelly!' mooed Teet. 'We want to pop out tonight to see if we can change it for a cream one!'

Bello jabbed the remote control again and Nelly watched in awe as a troupe of dancing Dendrilegs cancanned across the screen, singing a song about Lumpet sandwiches.

'That's the Dendrilegs Channel,' mooed Bello,

jabbing at the screen again. 'What else have we got?'

Weirdscreen had the lot. There were two hundred and fifty-seven channels available. If you liked tree throwing, mountain flattening, grenade swallowing, ceiling walking, slug cooking, tentacle wrestling, sucker problems, Veri farming, chat shows, splat shows, feeler puppets, health and ugliness, Squiddl racing, Nugg jumping, debates about Leems, Pipplewak history, 4D cartoons and pretty much anything weird really, Weirdscreen was the TV for you.

'Our telly packed up today,' said Nelly. 'We'll probably have to get a new one. Can you get *Summerdale Farm*?'

Bello shook his horns. 'No, we only get the normal channels, Nelly.'

Bello handed Nelly the remote control. 'Here we are, why don't yoooooooou have a little play?'

'If you want to go interactive, push the furry green button,' mooed Teet. 'I'm just going to run a brush through my udders and we'll be off.'

Petal watched her mum and dad leave the room and then rushed over to Nelly and gave her knees another big hug.

'Come and sit on the settee with me, Nelly!' she mooed. 'The Fuzzies are on in a minute!'

Nelly tottered across the floor in the direction of the settee and then *timberrred* on to the cream cushions. 'What channel is it?' she asked, staring at the two hundred and fifty-seven options.

'Channel 1,' mooed Petal.

'How doooooo I look?' mooed Teet from the doorway. Nelly turned to Teet with a nod of approval. She had parted her udders down the middle.

'We've left a bowl of num nums for you in the kitchen, Nelly. Petal has had her tea, and she's washed and cleaned her teeth. Can you make sure she's in bed by seven-thirty?'

'Will doooooo,' replied Nelly, with a click of button one.

'We'll be back by nine-thirty, probably earlier,' mooed Bello. 'Don't get oblong eyes!'

'We won't!' mooed Petal, ducking under the remote control and snuggling on to Nelly's lap. 'You're going to love the Fuzzies, Nelly! I know all the words to all the songs!'

'The Fuzzies it is, then!' smiled Nelly with a jab.

2

'There's a land
That should be banned –
Slimy dark
With sucking sand!
And it smells,
It really pongs –
Just the place
For singalongs!
Fuzzies!
Disgusting Fuzzies!
Stamp your hooves
And join the Fuzzies!
Blimmin' blimey,
Aren't we slimy,
Revolting, gross
And Grade A grimy!

Be a Fuzzy!
Let's get scuzzy!
It's Fuzzie time today –
Hooray!'

As Petal's head swayed happily to and fro in time to the music, Nelly stared at the screen in disbelief. The Fuzzies certainly weren't like any children's TV presenters she had ever seen.

'*Hello, children,*' said two large, grey fur-balls with harvest-spider-thin legs and bulbous bluebottle eyes. '*Today we're going to count tentacles. Would you like to count tentacles with us?*'

Nelly's chin began to tickle as Petal started nodding her head enthusiastically. Nelly craned her chin away from Petal's udders and stared as the fur-balls stepped to one side and were suddenly joined in the dark studio cave by a Dendrilegs, two Squiddls, a Squurm and a monster Nelly had never seen before.

'*Hello, children!*' they gurgled, kicking and

waving their tentacles like octopuses at a line dance.

'*Are you ready to sing a song about tentacles?*'

'Yeeessss!' chorused Petal, slipping off Nelly's lap and clip-clopping right up close up to the screen.

'*Here we go!*

I like tentacles, one, two, three!
See my tentacles waving free!
We like tentacles, four, five, six!
See our tentacles play some tricks!
Seven, eight tentacles smash your boat!
Nine, ten tentacles grip your throat!
Tangling tentacles
'Neath the seas!
Strangling tentacles
Squeeze, squeeze, squeeze!'

Nelly gulped. Both Squiddls lay dead on the floor of the studio cave and a plywood model of a boat lay in splinters.

'*Did you like that, children?*' growled the Fuzzies.

'Yeessssss!' mooed Petal, clonking her hooves together and giving her cucumber-green bottom a rhythmic little wiggle.

Nelly raised the remote control and jabbed it at the screen.

'What else is on?' she blustered.

'Ohhhhhh, don't turn it off, Nelly!' mooed Petal. 'I like the Fuzzies.'

'Yes, well I'm not sure the Fuzzies are suitable viewing for children,' said Nelly, flicking to another channel at random.

'But it's a children's programme!' protested Petal.

'That's beside the point,' argued Nelly.

Petal squeezed on to Nelly's lap again as Nelly began to flick randomly through the channels in search of some suitable viewing matter.

A large jellyfish with three ducks' beaks was being filleted on Channel 22. Two teams of Hojpogs were playing tug-of-war across a river of burning petrol on Channel 83.

A green face pack was being removed with a pickaxe from a Huffaluk on Channel 111. And a punch-up between three Pipplewaks had just broken out on the Peace Channel.

Goodness, thought Nelly, this makes *Summerdale Farm* look like *Songs of Praise*. She changed channel again and stared in disbelief. Every channel seemed to have a surprise in store.

'*Headsache?*' said a three-headed monster on Channel 222. He was holding up a fluorescent-yellow packet of tablets the size of cricket balls.

'Then try Noddl-eze. Fast acting and easy to swallow, Noddl-eze is the quick and easy way to rid all of your heads of headache and flu symptoms.'

A diagram of three heads instantly turned from red to green as a fast-acting tablet disappeared down a hairy windpipe and exploded like a grenade. '*It's a doddle with new Noddl-eze!*'

'Wow!' said Nelly. She'd never seen a monster TV commercial before.

'*Start your day the Disgustiflakes way!*' croaked

a toady-looking monster in pink pyjamas. '*Disgustiflakes are rich in iron, copper, aluminium and bite-size pieces of plastic. Mmmm – disgusting!*' he croaked again, raising a large spoonful to his lips and biting down hard with an earth-shattering crunch.

'I love Disgustiflakes,' mooed Petal. 'You get a free Spleep inside each packet.'

'What's a Spleep?' asked Nelly.

'It's a kind of disco maggot,' explained Petal.

'Great!' said Nelly, none the wiser.

For ten minutes or so Nelly surfed the Weirdscreen menu. There were so many channels to choose from, it was difficult to know where to start or finish.

She jabbed the remote control at the screen again and then again and again, finally plumping for the comedy channel. At least it was *called* the Comedy Channel . . .

Nelly stared straight-faced at a Gumbat standing on a stage, resting one tentacle on a microphone stand and holding two microphones to two of his mouths with another pair of tentacles.

'*Why did the Veri cross the road?*' he screeched with one mouth.

'*Because a Dendrilegs bought a new speedboat!*' replied the mouth above.

Petal rocked back with a snort, throwing Nelly backwards into the settee.

'What's so funny?' asked Nelly, a little winded.

'That joke was!' roared Petal.

Nelly raised her eyebrows and waited to be amused.

It was to be a long wait – in fact, to Nelly, Gumbat stand-up comedy seemed about as funny as being locked inside a broom cupboard with Asti.

'*What's the difference between a Pollimoke and a Jurzi?*' grinned one of the Gumbat's mouths.

'*A Pollimoke doesn't water the garden!*' quipped another.

Nelly stared blankly at the screen as the Gumbat rattled off twenty of the least funny jokes she had ever heard in her life, saving the worst for last.

'*My mother-in-law has got no nose,*' he squawked.

'*Oh really, how does she smell?*' enquired mouth two.

'*Like a caravan!*' quipped mouth three.

Petal threw her hooves into the air, doubled over with uncontrollable hysteria and then roared like a Borkybine.

Nelly sat on the settee solemnly. 'I don't get it,' she said. 'I don't get any of it.'

Petal certainly did get it; in fact, she was in danger of splitting her sides. Her face had turned white, her cheeks had turned yellow and her eyes had begun watering like tinned lychees.

With a gasp, a cough and then a GARGANTUAN wheeze, she reeled forward and exploded into the splutter of all splutters. She spluttered so loud and with such force that a large object suddenly fired from her mouth, bounced off the far wall, and clattered on to the carpet!

Nelly peered across the floor at the mystery projectile. It was about the size of a golf ball, smooth and white but with three jagged prongs at one end.

'My tooooooth!' mooed Petal, wiping tears of laughter from her eyes with her hooves. 'My toooooth has come out, Nelly!'

'You must have laughed it loose!' smiled Nelly, finally finding something to chuckle about. 'Good job it wasn't a funny joke! *All* your teeth might have fallen out!'

Petal wiggled her tongue through the hole that the tooth had left.

'It *was* a funny joke, Nelly. It was a *very* funny joke,' she mooed.

'I'll take your word for it,' said Nelly, forgetting about the TV for a moment and retrieving the tooth from the carpet. It was quite a sizeable lump, as white as snow and as smooth as china.

'It's a moolar,' said Petal. 'Dad says all Cowcumber teeth are called moolars.'

'You should put it under your pillow tonight,'

said Nelly, placing the tooth on the cream marble mantelpiece.

'Why?' mooed Petal.

'If you put it under your pillow the tooth fairy might come and leave you some money!' said Nelly. 'I got two pounds for two teeth wunth,' she said, running her tongue over her teeth again.

'Mummy and Daddy have never told me about that,' said Petal. 'They always throw my old teeth away.'

'Well,' smiled Nelly, checking she had a bit of loose change in her pocket, 'we'll put your tooth under the pillow tonight and see what happens.'

Petal smiled broadly. The gap in her teeth looked like a mousehole.

Nelly picked up the remote control again and pointed it in the direction of the Weirdscreen. 'I'll try my lucky number,' she said, tapping a three and an eight out with her finger and hoping for the best.

The screen sparkled pink momentarily before cutting dramatically to reveal a Water Greep wearing a lemon and gold stripy tutu. With a graceful flap of its webbed feet and a barrelling wave of its arms, the Water Greep hopped gracefully across a stage, straight into the outstretched arms of a Hojpog dressed in a sparkling silver tutu.

'It's ballet!' gasped Nelly. 'Monster ballet!'

'It's *bull*et,' mooed Petal, as the Hojpog suddenly flexed its bristles, hit the Water Greep on the head with a frying pan and then rolled up into a ball.

Petal was right. It was bullying, to classical music.

Nelly watched in stunned disbelief as the camera pulled wide to reveal a huge, white, wrestling canvas studded with sequins. The ring was cordoned with golden ropes and in one corner a full Grimp orchestra was playing violins.

'The last one standing wins,' mooed Petal.

The music from the orchestra suddenly swelled as the Water Greep staggered dizzily across the canvas and fell headlong out of the ring. As its flippers tumbled out of view, a Dendrilegs dressed in a crimson taffeta tutu slithered under the ropes. To Nelly's horror it was carrying two baseball bats!

'This is like *WWF Wrestling* and *Come Dancing* all rolled into in one!' gasped Nelly.

'Yoooou can join in if yoooou like!' mooed Petal.

Nelly's eyes averted to the bottom right-hand corner of the Weirdscreen where the words *Press furry green button for interactive action* had suddenly appeared.

Nelly looked at Petal. Her first instinct was to ignore it. 'I'm not very up on technology,' murmured Nelly.

'Just push the furry green button,' mooed Petal, encouragingly. 'It's easy.'

Nelly's fingers paused and then crept like a spider across the cream settee and casually picked up the remote control.

'Shall I?' she said to Petal.

'Yethh!' nodded Petal.

Nelly wavered for a split second, poised her index finger over the furry green button on the remote and then pressed down firmly.

The instant she pressed the furry green button, the picture vanished.

'Where did everyone go?' asked Nelly, staring blankly at the furry green button.

'May I have this dance, madam?' dribbled a suckery, thwuckery voice from behind her.

Nelly wheeled round to find the Dendrilegs in the crimson tutu standing right behind her! Not only that, the full Grimp orchestra had assembled in the hallway and the Hojpog in the silver tutu was practising dance combat moves over by the French windows!

Nelly's jaw dropped like a drawbridge as the Dendrilegs curtsied politely and then handed her a baseball bat.

Nelly dropped the baseball bat on to the carpet immediately and tried to reason her way out of the predicament.

'Sorry, there's been a mistake,' she flustered. 'Bullying isn't my thing,' she explained. 'Actually, neither is ballet.'

The four eyes of the Dendrilegs stared at the floor and then turned to the Hojpog. This wasn't going to be easy.

'I didn't realise what interactive meant, you see,' said Nelly. 'I just pushed the furry green button, not knowing what was going to happen.'

The orchestra raised their violins to their chins

and the Dendrilegs raised his baseball bat to head height.

'Nelly! Nelly! Nelly! Nelly!' cheered Petal encouragingly from the sidelines.

'Let the performance commence!' cackled the Hojpog.

Nelly ducked sharply as the Dendrilegs took a swipe at her with his bat and then began chasing her round the settee.

'Oh no!' gasped Nelly. 'What have I done?'

As she circled the settee for the second time, her eyes pinged to the cream vases on the mantelpiece.

'Nooo!' cried Nelly. 'You mustn't! Not in here! You'll break something!'

She ducked sharply again as the Dendrilegs took another swing at her.

'Will you stop clapping and do something, Petal!' she gasped, glancing over her shoulder.

Petal had begun to WHOOOOOOOP loudly. The Hojpog had joined in the chase as well and was now pirouetting in hot pursuit across the cushions.

Nelly ducked low and snatched up the remote

control from the cushions. There had to be some way to stop this. She was going to get clobbered if there wasn't. She pointed the remote over her shoulder and pressed the furry green button down hard, trying to zap everyone back to the Weirdscreen.

'They're catching you up, Nelly!' clapped Petal excitedly.

Nelly whip-panned her head backwards and groaned. Pushing the furry green button was having no effect at all!

She tried the red button. But everything in the room turned black and white.

She tried the white button. But everything and everyone suddenly switched to slow motion.

'Please be the yellow button!' she gasped, momentarily freeze-framing her assailants in mid-pas de deux.

'How do I get rid of them, Petal?' gasped Nelly, jabbing the pink button as she circled the settee for the tenth time. 'I'm running out of buttons to try!'

Petal broke from her cheerleading for a moment and pointed at the remote with her hoof.

'Sorry, Nelly,' she mooed. 'I thought you were having a good time! Push the furry green button TWICE!'

Nelly pointed the remote over her shoulder again and jab-jabbed the furry green button in rapid succession.

In a flash, her tutu-clad assailants vanished from the lounge and returned to the plasma screen on the wall.

Nelly stared at the Weirdscreen and watched with a shudder as the Hojpog pounced on the Dendrilegs, dragging its tutu round its knees. With a pirouette and a leap, the Hojpog waved to the audience, grabbed the Dendrilegs by the tentacles, swung him around his head and hurled him over the ropes and out of the ring. The music climaxed, the audience went wild and the Hojpog acknowledged victory with a teary-eyed twirl.

Nelly flopped back into the settee.

'That's the last time I go interactive, I can tell

you,' she puffed. 'Why didn't you tell me that was going to happen?'

'Haven't you got interactive at home?' mooed Petal apologetically.

'Yes, but not that inter and not that active!' protested Nelly.

'I thought you were enjoying yourself,' mooed Petal.

Nelly blew hard. She could feel her heart pumping inside her chest.

'Never mind,' she said, glancing wearily at her watch. 'That's enough telly for now.' She turned the Weirdscreen off and hid the remote control safely under the cushions. 'I think it's time you went up to bed, Petal. I really do.'

Petal grinned a mousehole and jumped down from the settee. 'Weirdscreen is brilliant, isn't it, Nelly?' she mooed. 'Doooo you wish yoooooou had it at home?'

Nelly puffed out her cheeks and shook her head. 'I'll stick to *Summerdale*, thanks,' she smiled.

3

'Will you bring my toooooth upstairs with yoooou?' mooed Petal.

'Yes, I'll bring your tooth,' smiled Nelly.

Nelly carried Petal's tooth up the stairs and waited outside the bathroom door while she polished it.

'I want to make it nice for the toooooth fairy,' mooed Petal excitedly.

Petal held the moolar in her hoof and then carefully squeezed the last drop of toothpaste from the tube. Nelly watched in amazement as the squeeze of toothpaste slithered like a small worm across the tooth and began rubbing itself up, down and around the tooth in small, circular motions.

'Don't monsters need toothbrushes?' asked Nelly.

'No,' mooed Petal, 'the tooooothpaste does all the work.'

Nelly watched with interest as the green and blue stripy toothpaste worm worked itself into a froth before fizzling out into a squib of nothing.

'All done,' mooed Petal, rinsing the moolar under the tap and drying it with a cream hoof towel.

'OK, it's time you got into bed now, Petal,' smiled Nelly.

Petal clip-clopped happily out of the cream-tiled bathroom, down the cream-carpeted landing and into her bedroom.

'Put your tooth under here,' said Nelly, lifting up a cream pillow and patting the cream bed sheet below it. Petal placed the moolar carefully on to the sheet and watched excitedly as Nelly covered it with the pillow.

'It's still there!' said Petal, lifting the pillow immediately.

'Of course it's still there!' laughed Nelly. 'Tooth Fairies don't arrive that fast!'

Petal climbed into bed and pulled the cream duvet cover up to her chin.

'Those are my Spleeps,' she mooed, nodding towards the window.

Nelly patted the pillow into place and walked over to the cream-glossed window sill. Arranged carefully in a line were a collection of grey plastic maggots with matchstick-thin arms and legs. All of them seemed to be striking a variety of frozen disco-dance poses.

'How many are there in the set?' she asked, picking one of the Spleeps up and then dropping it immediately to the floor.

'It wriggled!' she cried.

It was true. The moment Nelly's fingers had touched the Spleep, a tune had begun to play from deep inside it and its body had begun to writhe like a maggot in time to the beat.

The music played for a few seconds and then cut out, freezing the Spleep into an alternative disco pose.

'A hundred,' mooed Petal. 'I only need eighty-nine more!'

'That's a lot of Disgustiflakes you're going to have to eat!' said Nelly, returning the Spleep to the window sill and watching it wriggle and writhe into an 'In da House' dance groove pose.

'I eat two boxes every morning,' mooed Petal.

'If you get any swaps, can I have them?' laughed Nelly. 'I'd love to put one down my sister's jumper!'

Nelly drew the cream curtains and kissed Petal on the forehead.

'Sleep well,' she said.

'I will,' yawned Petal, waving fondly to Nelly as she closed the bedroom door behind her.

Nelly patted the back pocket of her jeans as she walked down the stairs.

I'll wait till Petal is asleep and then I'll pop back up and slip 50p under her pillow, she thought to herself.

Actually, I'd better make it a pound – it's such a big tooth!

She walked into the lounge with a gap of her own to fill.

'Where's that bowl of num nums?' she wondered. 'I'm starving.'

Nelly liked crisps. But she REALLY liked Toot and Bello's num nums. They were the crispiest crisps she had ever munched or crunched. Every bite of a num num sent tremors through her jaw and a mini explosion reverberating through her brain. They were tasty, too. On her first visit to the Cowcumbers she had tried pirrin and ug flavour. She wasn't exactly sure what a pirrin or an ug were but she was pretty sure one of them was related to the strawberry family, if that was possible.

She walked into the cream kitchen and found a full bowl of metre-long spiral-shaped num nums waiting for her on the counter. From a distance they looked like dried potato peelings but close up they tasted like barley sugar.

'Mmm – delicious,' she muttered, crunching her way, helter-skelter fashion, from the top of one spiral to the bottom.

'I wonder what flavour these are,' she mused, picking up the empty packet that had been left on the side.

They were '*Num nums, lightly seasoned with fudd.*'

With a nod of approval, she picked up the bowl and returned to the lounge.

Nelly sighed contentedly. It was peace at last. Peace, telly and num nums.

She placed the bowl beside her on the settee and slid her fingers under the cushion.

The taste of fudd detonated deliciously on her tongue as she raised the TV remote to the screen. Taking extra special care to avoid the furry green button, she clicked firmly.

A crazy spectrum of colours rainbowed the width of the wall again and Channel 245 suddenly flickered into view.

Nelly had found the Pet Channel.

A Huffaluk vet appeared to be standing in a surgery, staring intently at an X-ray of a Gog's stomach. He couldn't be sure without exploratory surgery, but it looked like the Gog had swallowed the wheel of a car.

The Huffaluk dangled his single eye expertly over the X-ray and then prescribed a two-week course of tablets.

'*To be taken three times a day between wheels – I mean meals,*' he growled.

Next up was a breed of monster that Nelly had never seen before. It had two orange heads, huge jaws and a crunching headache.

'*How long has he been like this?*' asked the Huffaluk vet, tapping both of the monster's heads with a tuning fork.

'*Since Thursday,*' wheezed the Plook owner. '*He swallowed my portable hi-fi whole when I wasn't looking, and it was Saturday before the batteries ran down and the music stopped playing.*'

'*No wonder he's got a headache,*' growled the vet. '*I don't suppose he's had a wink of sleep.*'

'*None of us has,*' wheezed the Plook. '*The left-hand speaker has been blasting out through this jaw here and the right-hand speaker has been full blast out of the other jaw.*'

The Huffaluk stroked the hairs on his chin and then patted the monster pet tenderly on the back. '*I'm going to give you a little injection that will cure your taste in music,*' he growled.

The pet nodded both heads gratefully and then blinked with surprise as a needle attached to a steel bicycle pump went to work on his bottom.

Nelly unleashed another num num on her tongue and settled back into the settee to see what kind of pet would be brought into the surgery next.

'I know what that pet is called!' she said, with a crunch. 'It's a Shredda!'

Sure enough, a Pipplewak was walking into the surgery with all four wings wrapped around a glass bowl.

Inside the bowl, a Shredda was swimming around upside down and panting heavily.

Poor thing, thought Nelly. I wonder what the matter with it is?

She pointed the remote at the Weirdscreen and

eased up the volume. It was hard to hear what was being said above the crunch of her num nums.

'*She hasn't eaten for days!*' hooted the Pipplewak.

The vet opened the surgery freezer cabinet and took out what looked like a frozen leg of rhino. With a soft growl of encouragement, he dangled it over the bowl.

'*Here, girl, come and get your lumpit,*' he coaxed.

Nelly crunched down hard again as the Shredda flapped its crimson fins weakly and sank to the bottom of the bowl.

The Huffaluk vet stooped low and dangled his eye in a three hundred and sixty-degree circle around the bowl.

'*I'm afraid gonegreen has set in,*' he growled. '*Can you see the tip of those tails?*'

The Pipplewak stood on tiptoe and peered through the glass.

'*Oh yes,*' he hooted. '*They've gone green.*'

'*It's not good news, I'm afraid,*' growled the Huffaluk. '*I'm afraid she's going to need a triple tail transplant.*'

Nelly demolished another num num as the Pipplewak went weak at the knees and steadied itself on the chair.

A dramatic silence fell over the surgery as the cameras moved in to milk the moment.

Nelly munched and crunched some more and then reached into the bowl for another spiral.

'*Next!*' growled the Huffaluk, ever-conscious of the fact that the show must go on.

The Pipplewak and the Shredda were ushered out through the back door and what looked like a parrot with a bandaged trunk was carried in by a veterinary assistant.

'What sort of monster do you call that?' gasped Nelly.

It was a Pollyphant.

Nelly slowed the tempo of her munching.

'And what on earth is that?' she murmured to herself.

She retuned her senses for a moment, giving maximum sway to her ears.

She could hear something. Something strange, something weird.

And it wasn't coming from the Weirdscreen.

She dropped the unfinished num num back into the bowl and, with a slightly uneasy feeling, picked up the remote control. She stopped her munching and turned the volume on the Weirdscreen to mute.

The noise was coming from upstairs.

'PETAL!' she cried, leaping off the settee. Something was the matter with Petal!

4

Moos of distress were coming from Petal's bedroom. They were growing louder by the second, so loud, in fact, that the cream chandelier on the upstairs landing had begun to shake. Nelly added to the tremors by charging up the stairs like a Lumpit. With a breathless 'Coming, Petal!' she raced across the landing and sprung the handle on Petal's bedroom door.

'It's OK, Nelly's here! It's only a bad dream!'

Nelly barged into the bedroom and slammed immediately into shock.

Her heart leapt like a stunt bike and her mind spun into freefall.

It was much worse than a bad dream. It was much worse than a nightmare. It was a monster from hell.

To Nelly's horror, a venomous creature with dragonfly wings was hanging by its claws from Petal's headboard. It had hold of Petal's face and was trying to prise open her mouth. Petal was struggling hard to get free but the creature's three-fingered paws had hold of her like a vice. As Nelly entered the bedroom it looked up at her and glared. Nelly stared back, unable to believe what she was seeing. It had the frame of a gibbon but its bony arms and legs were spiked like monkey-puzzle-tree branches and its coat was matted with grey fur. Nelly blinked darkly into its terrifying, green, saucer-sized eyes and then wilted at the sight of its teeth. Black and white they were, arranged alternately across its jaws like wonky piano keys.

For the first time in her life, Nelly actually froze with fear. She couldn't move. Every atom in her body had turned to ice. All she could do was stand and stare. She couldn't think. She could barely breathe.

Petal was kicking her bedsheets wildly. She had

her lips shut tight for fear of the creature but was willing Nelly to move with her eyes. The creature followed Petal's gaze, reared its head contemptuously and spat like a camel. Nelly winced as a bullet of yellow spittle winged the sleeve of her favourite sweatshirt.

Now, if there's one thing Nelly didn't like it was spitting. It wasn't a prudy thing or a girly thing, it was a manners thing. Nelly knew girls at school who spat, but believe you me, they never spat at her.

Nelly unfroze. The ice shattered, her temper snapped.

'GET OFF MY PETAL – YOU FREAK!' she shouted, rushing towards the bed. The piano teeth bared themselves again, but there was no stopping Nelly now. With an angry caveman roar, she grabbed the creature by the scruff of its neck and hurled it bravely into the curtains.

Eleven different disco tunes struck up simultaneously as the Spleep collection scattered across the window ledge and tumbled on to the carpet.

The creature crumpled on to the floor, looking like a motorway road-kill, but then staggered to its feet with a shriek. Nelly wasted no time. She snatched Petal out of the bed and whisked her out through the bedroom door.

Placing her safely on the landing carpet she doubled back, grabbed the door handle and slammed it shut.

As the door swung to, a grey, wolf-like claw tried to hook itself around the middle of the door to prevent her from closing it, but Nelly had summoned the strength of ten Huffaluks. With a howl of pain, the claw splintered and the door wedged tight in the frame.

'Help me, Petal, you've got to help me,' cried Nelly. 'We mustn't let it escape from your room!'

Petal stepped nervously towards the door. She still wouldn't speak for fear of losing her teeth. 'Where do your mum and dad keep the key?' gasped Nelly, straining to keep the door closed.

Petal pointed her hoof up above the door

frame, where the key was kept out of reach.

Nelly's arms felt ready to snap. She had both hands clamped to the door handle and her full bodyweight was straining at forty-five degrees.

She knew she couldn't hang on for much longer. If she wanted to reach the key, she would have to risk letting go with one hand.

Her wrists shook violently as the creature hurled itself at the door from the other side.

It was shredding the door like a cougar at a scratching post.

'What sort of monster is it?' whispered Nelly.

'I don't know,' mooed Petal, 'but it wanted my teeth. I said it could have the one under my pillow but it wanted all of them. Even the ones in my mouth!'

Nelly gasped and then shook her head. It couldn't be. It just couldn't possibly be a tooth fairy . . . could it?

'I'm going to try and lock the door, Petal. On the count of three, grab the handle and pull with all your might.'

Petal nodded and then wavered as the door frame shuddered again.

'Trust me, Petal,' said Nelly. 'Watch my lips and make your move on three.'

Petal watched Nelly's lips mime the three count.

On the third nod, Nelly let go of the handle with her right hand and swiftly reached up above her head. As her fingers scrabbled blindly across the top of the door frame, Petal gripped the handle with both hooves and arched her green cucumber back to breaking point.

Suddenly the handle began to bend. It was being forced downwards with awesome pressure from the other side.

'Quick!' squeaked Petal. 'I can't hold it.'

Nelly lunged for the key with the tips of her fingers and then gasped in dismay as the key tumbled from its ledge and clattered to the base of the door.

Her eyes fell with it and then widened as a wolfish claw poked out from underneath the door and hooked itself through the circular eye at the top of the key.

'Grab it, Petal!' Nelly cried, stamping down hard on the key before it could slide out of sight. 'Grab the key before it takes it!'

Petal dropped to her knees and prised the key from the tip of the creature's talon.

'I've got it!' she mooed. 'What now?'

Nelly snatched the key from Petal's hoof, rammed it into the keyhole and twisted hard. With a click and a howl, the door was finally secured.

Nelly placed her back against the door and slid down on to her bum.

'Now,' she panted, 'now, Petal, we ring for help.'

5

Lump and Poltis were sitting down to dinner with their Dendrileg children, Bog and Blotch, when the phone rang.

'I wonder who that could be,' thwucked Lump, popping a spoonful of weeps into his mouth and chewing thoughtfully.

'Well, if you don't answer it you won't find out,' said Poltis, cutting the children's boshburgers into triangles.

Lump looked ruefully at his plate and then left the table with a sigh.

'It better be important,' he grumbled with a suckery thwuck.

Poltis and the twins watched from the dinner table as Lump wriggled across the carpet, lifted the phone from the shelf and held it to his fourth ear.

'Nelly! How lovely to hear from you!' he thwucked.

Poltis, Bog and Blotch looked at Lump as the colour ran from his face.

'Oh no! Nelly, you mustn't . . . you haven't . . . there isn't . . .'

Lump winced and turned to his wife.

'But you've managed to lock the door . . . ? Then keep it locked. Don't for ANY reason go back into Petal's room. If you do you'll be eating soup for the rest of your life!'

Lump put the phone down and stared ashen-faced at Poltis.

'Nelly's in trouble. BIG trouble,' he whispered. 'I need to go to her straight away.'

'But what about your dinner?' asked Poltis.

'I've lost my appetite,' thwucked Lump.

Poltis left the table and followed her husband to the door.

'Whatever is it?' she whispered, not wanting to alarm the children any more than they already were.

Lump placed two tentacles on his wife's shoulder and shuddered.

'It's a Tooth Furry.'

6

Lump arrived at the front door of 11 Parma Drive in double quick time, his tentacles flapping like footballers' shoelaces.

Nelly and Petal were waiting for him on the front step, as far from Petal's bedroom as they could get without actually leaving the house.

Lump put his tentacles around them protectively and walked them back into the lounge.

'Nelly, it's bad news,' he thwucked. 'Nice telly, by the way.'

Petal smiled and nodded but Nelly sat down on the settee with a frown.

'You put a tooth under Petal's pillow, didn't you?' thwucked Lump, trying not to sound too critical.

'Yes, but we always do that in my house if Asti or I lose a tooth. If you do it in our house the tooth fairy comes when you're asleep and swaps the tooth for some money,' said Nelly, springing to her own defence. 'Actually, it's not really a tooth fairy, it's a mum or a dad. Tooth fairies aren't real.'

Lump slapped a tentacle to his forehead and closed all four eyes.

'If a monster loses a tooth we put it in the bin and screw down the lid. We never, ever put it under a pillow. If you put a monster tooth under your pillow the worst possible thing will happen.'

Nelly braced herself for the bad news.

Lump opened his silver-grey eyes and shook his head gravely.

'You get a TOOTH FURRY in your bedroom. Nelly. Not a tooth *fairy* or a mum or a dad. You get a spitting, snarling, hate-filled monster with only one thing on its mind. *Your teeth.* A Tooth Furry will not leave your house until it has filled its sack with your teeth.'

Nelly squirmed in her seat. 'But my teeth aren't wobbly,' she said, giving them a quick once-over with her tongue.

'Neither are mine,' mooed Petal.

'The Tooth Furry doesn't care if they are wobbly or not. He'll prise your lips open and wrench your teeth right out by the roots!' thwucked Lump. 'Before you know it, you'll have nothing but gums left.'

Nelly looked at the bowl of num nums and shuddered. How could she possibly suck a num num? It didn't bear thinking about.

'Well, the good news is we've got a grown-up Dendrilegs here to help us!' said Nelly, trying to find a bright side to look on.

'And the bad news is, I don't know how to get rid of it,' sighed Lump.

'Oh,' said Nelly.

Petal, Lump and Nelly sat in silence for a moment and pondered their predicament.

'Do you think Grit would know?' said Nelly, pulling her mobile phone out of her pocket and preparing to ring her Huffaluk friend at Number 42.

'No monster knows,' thwucked Lump in an unnervingly defeated tone.

Nelly slid the phone back into her pocket. She looked at Petal and offered her a num num. Petal declined the offer.

'I've already cleaned my teeth,' she mooed.

'Well, we're going to have to get rid of it somehow,' said Nelly, flopping back miserably into the settee. 'I don't think Teet and Bello will be at all pleased to have Petal sharing her bedroom with a Tooth Furry.'

Lump flopped back too, and began wringing his tentacles into anxious knots.

'Couldn't yoooou ask him to go nicely?' mooed Petal.

'Tooth Furries don't know the meaning of nice,' thwucked Lump.

'What do they want with all those teeth, anyway?' asked Nelly.

'Dentures,' said Lump. 'Tooth Furry teeth are

so black and so rotten, they are always on the hunt for new ones.'

'The Tooth Furry in my room had black and white teeth,' mooed Petal.

'The white ones were false,' thwucked Lump.

'Has anyone here got any teeth they don't need?' said Nelly, clutching at the flimsiest of straws.

'Nope,' thwucked Lump.

'Me neither,' mooed Petal.

'What do you think the Tooth Furry is doing right now?' said Nelly, peering up at the ceiling. 'I can't hear it. Perhaps it's gone away.'

Lump wrung his tentacles into a triple-sheepshank double-hitch knot and shook his head.

'He'll be simmering, fuming, cursing and waiting. Believe me, Nelly, he won't have gone away.'

'He better not be playing with my Spleeps!' mooed Petal indignantly.

Nelly smiled. The very thought of a Tooth

Furry at a disco was too much to conjure with.

'Right!' said Nelly, standing up, smoothing her sweatshirt and adjusting her scrunchee. 'If he won't go, then I'll jolly well make him go. I'm going to go up there, pick him up by the scruff of the neck and boot him out of the front door!'

Lump spluttered and then sprung off the settee after her. 'No, Nelly! You mustn't go up there, it's too dangerous.'

But Nelly was already out of the door and halfway up the stairs. Lump dived across the hallway carpet and wrapped a tentacle around her ankle, but Nelly kicked her foot free.

'Enough's enough,' said Nelly crossly. 'And I'll tell you another thing. If he spits at me again, I'll punch all his white teeth out!'

It was fighting talk, and an angry Nelly was a formidable adversary for sure. But Lump knew what she was getting herself into and genuinely feared for her safety. He bounded up the stairs behind her and caught up with her on the landing. She already had her hand on the handle of Petal's bedroom door and was about to turn the key.

'If you're going in, I'm going in!' gasped Lump with a nervous thwuckery, thwuck, thwuck.

Nelly turned to Lump with her eyes blazing. 'Let's do it!' she said.

Petal watched anxiously from the top of the stairs as Nelly turned the key of the bedroom door. With a look of steely determination, she slowly eased down the handle and then barged into the room. Screaming like a Ninja and thwucking like a Dendrilegs, the two of them bundled across the floor and tumbled on to the bed. Nelly wasted no time, leaping up from the cream duvet and then wheeling round with a high kick that she had seen someone do in a kung-fu movie. Her outstretched trainer scythed impressively through the air but connected with nothing. Lump, meanwhile, reared up on to one tentacle and began waving the other three like a hydra.

At nothing. Nelly and Lump looked around the bedroom. The Tooth Furry was nowhere to be seen.

Lump dropped his tentacles with relief and sat down on the bed. Nelly lowered her trainer to the floor and punched the air with delight.

'He's gone! He's gone, Lump. I told you he would go!'

Petal clip-clopped nervously up to her bedroom door and peered inside. She found Lump and Nelly dancing a celebratory highland fling around her bedroom.

'He's gone! He's gone! He's gone! He's gone!' they sang.

'He hasn't been playing with my Spleeps, has he?' mooed Petal, jealously.

Nelly stopped dancing and looked happily at the curtains. The Spleeps were lined up neatly along the window sill.

'They're all there, Petal!' she laughed.

'Thanks for picking them up off the floor, Nelly,' mooed Petal.

Nelly shook her head. 'I didn't pick them up. Did you pick them up, Lump?'

Lump shook his head.

'How many Spleeps did you say you had?' asked Nelly, beginning to count them.

'Eleven,' mooed Petal.

Nelly scratched her head. 'Well, there are seventeen there now.'

Petal, Nelly and Lump stared at the window sill. There were six new Spleeps poking out from the bottom of the curtains.

'Those aren't Spleeps,' thwucked Lump, slowly backing away towards the open bedroom door. 'They're CLAWS!'

Nelly recoiled in horror as the curtains in the window suddenly flew back and the dreadful, drooling piano teeth of the Tooth Furry loomed large.

'Run, Petal!' Nelly cried, as a bullet of yellow spittle whistled past her ear.

'I'm gone!' mooed Petal, turning tail and stampeding towards the door.

Lump turned to run with her but before he had managed one step, the Tooth Furry had sprung from the window ledge and fastened itself to his face.

'Isgotme!' squawked Lump, trying his best to speak without opening his mouth.

Nelly watched in horror as Lump and the Tooth Furry became an unpickable knot of tentacles and matted fur. Things weren't going to plan at all.

'GET OFF LUMP THIS MINUTE, ASHTRAY GOB!' shouted Nelly, jumping into the fray and trying her best to wrestle the Tooth Furry's fingers away from Lump's lips.

The Tooth Furry turned angrily towards Nelly and unleashed another bullet of spittle. Nelly ducked to avoid it, bared her own teeth fearlessly and snarled a tiger growl.

'So you want to play dirty, do you?' she roared, forcing her index finger into the Tooth Furry's nose and pushing upwards as hard as she could.

The Tooth Furry howled like a wolverine and loosened its grip on Lump's lips. Its green saucer eyes watered and then disappeared behind pale, veined eyelids.

'They don't like it up 'em!' roared Nelly, sensing that her nasal assault was paying off.

'Get ready to run, Lump!'

The Tooth Furry squirmed and then reared backwards as Nelly brandished her other index finger.

With a squelch and a pop, her first finger came free. Its nostril smarting and its emerald eyes watering, the Tooth Furry recoiled on to the bed.

Nelly stood her ground, brandishing both of her index fingers like daggers. She had the upper hand in every sense of the word, but was doubtful how long it would last.

'Do we fight or do we run?' said Nelly.

'I'm for running!' thwacked Lump, heading for the door.

With a parting growl, Nelly wheeled round and sprinted hard after Lump. The outstretched claws of the Tooth Furry clipped the back of her trainers as she leapt into the hall.

'Shut the door, Lump, shut the door!' she cried, tripping on to the hallway floor.

With lightning dexterity, Lump slammed the

door behind her, forced the key into the lock, wrenched his tentacle hard round and secured the door.

Petal's bedroom door reverberated as a tornado of fury launched itself at it from the other side.

'I don't think he's happy,' thwucked Lump.

'I think you're right,' panted Nelly.

'What's that on your finger?' mooed Petal.

'Don't ask,' groaned Nelly.

Petal and Lump waited at the top of the stairs as Nelly nipped into the bathroom to dispose of the monster bogey that had attached itself to her fingernail.

She emerged a couple of moments later with hands smelling of cream soap and a mind set on victory.

'We need a new plan,' she said. 'Let's regroup in the lounge.'

Nelly, Petal and Lump sat on the settee and stared blankly at the wall.

'Do you think, perhaps, that if we called the police, they would come and arrest it?' suggested Nelly.

Lump shook his head. 'Not unless you want a toothless police force,' he thwucked.

'How about the army?' said Nelly.

'Same problem,' thwucked Lump.

Nelly looked at her watch. It was half-past eight and the Cowcumbers had said they might be home early.

'So let's go through this again,' she said, turning to Lump. 'There's a Tooth Furry in Petal's bedroom and no amount of persuasion will make him leave – correct?'

'Only a sackful of teeth will persuade him to leave,' thwucked Lump.

Petal crossed her hooves and sighed.

'But we haven't got a sackful of teeth, we've only got one, and he's already nabbed it,' she mooed.

Nelly leant back into the settee and frowned.

Lump draped his tentacles over the arm and sighed.

Petal made herself more comfortable and succumbed to the num nums.

'I've got it!' cried Nelly, skating the palm of her hand across the settee and then sending it for a foray beneath the cushions.

Her fingers emerged, clutching the Weirdscreen remote control.

'This is hardly the time to be watching telly,' thwucked Lump.

'This is EXACTLY the time to be watching telly!' insisted Nelly, jabbing the remote at the screen.

The spectrum of colours did their Weirdscreen thing and Channel 93 burst into life.

'Ooh, good,' thwucked Lump, 'it's *Strange Hill.* I used to watch that when I was at school.'

'Well, you can't watch it now,' said Nelly, flicking to Channel 94.

'Shockey!' mooed Petal. 'I want to be a shockey player when I'm older.'

A plutonium-coated puck flew across a dry-ice shockey rink, but before it could explode, Nelly changed channel again to reveal a Glooble lying on a couch having potato peelings cemented to his head. It was the Muck-over Channel. Nelly flicked again.

Now it was *Beastenders,* now it was the raspberry-infested Fartoon Channel and now it was an ad for tentacle polish.

'Come on,' said Nelly, jab-jab-jabbing at the screen. 'You must be there somewhere.'

Petal and Lump looked at each other and shrugged their shoulders. The Weirdsceen channels were flashing past so fast it was beginning to make them giddy.

Nelly moved to the edge of her seat and concentrated hard.

'*Take one fresh yelk,*' hooted a chef on Channel 106.

'*Tonight, Mutthew, I'm going to be a paving slab,*' growled a grey lump of a creature on Channel 107.

'*Darling, your eyes are like gog plops,*' squeaked a Qityr on the Romance Channel.

Nelly huffed and puffed and then glanced sidelong at Petal and Lump. 'Sorry, guys,' she said, 'but I'm looking for something very particular.'

It wasn't *The Nine O'Clock Newts.*

It wasn't *Slimewatch.*

Or an ad for horn extensions.

Or an ad for spike clippers.

It wasn't a programme about belly-button fungus.

Or a debate about swamp fleas.

Lump and Petal looked up at the ceiling. The

cream lampshade above their heads was beginning to shake. 'I think the Tooth Furry is trying to bust out,' thwucked Lump.

'I know, I know,' muttered Nelly, continuing to surf every channel. She knew she was running out of time.

'Gotcha!' she cried, slamming the pause button on the remote control.

It was an ad for Kritter-fix denture paste.

'Cross your hooves and tentacles,' said Nelly hopefully.

Lump and Petal watched as Nelly pointed the remote control at the Weirdscreen and then placed her finger on the furry green button.

'Here goes,' she said, pressing the furry green button down hard.

Petal and Lump jumped back in their seats as a Squurm with silver-grey feelers suddenly appeared in the lounge before them. He was holding three walking sticks with three feelers, seven different sets of dentures in seven feelers and a toothbrush and a tube of Kritter-fix dental paste with two others.

'*Hi there!*' he squawked insincerely, fixing Nelly, Petal and Lump with a brighter than bright white smile. '*When you get to a certain age and your teeth start to give up on you, it's important to have a denture toothpaste that's there for you one hundred per cent.*'

'Yes, yes, very interesting,' said Nelly, standing up and gently leading the Squurm out of the lounge and towards the stairs.

'*A denture paste that you can rely on . . .*'

'Yes, yes,' yawned Nelly. 'Now then, this way, mind the steps.'

'*A denture paste that's your friend,*' squawked the Squurm, following Nelly up the stairs.

'Everyone needs a friend,' said Nelly.

'*Kritter-fix is a friend to every kind of denture,*' squawked the Squurm, holding up seven different varieties of monster denture. '*Whether you have the large, grinding teeth of a Huffaluk, the small nibbling teeth of a Qityr, or the strange goofy teeth of my Dendrilegs friend here,*' he said, turning to Mump who was following them up the stairs.

'What does he mean, goofy?' squawked Lump indignantly as they reached the top of the stairs.

'*Kritter-fix is a friend to every kind of monster. It's the monster denture paste you can trust, see!*'

The Squurm placed two feelers inside his mouth and tugged hard.

'He does go on a bit, doesn't he?' mooed Petal, following close behind Lump.

'*There's no budging a denture fixed with Kritter-fix!*' smiled the Squurm, holding up the tube for all to admire.

'I wouldn't count on it,' whispered Nelly, under her breath.

'*And now there's New Kritter-fix Plus!*' squawked the Squurm, producing a completely different tube seemingly from nowhere.

Nelly placed the key in Petal's bedroom door and smiled.

'Don't tell us, tell him,' she said, opening the door, pushing the Squurm gently inside and quickly locking it again.

Mayhem broke out immediately. It was World War Three striped with fluoride. Bangs and crashes and squawks and squeaks exploded from every corner of the room.

Nelly, Petal and Lump tried to put their ears to

the door, but the noises coming from the other side were so loud that they ended up having to cover them with their tentacles, hooves and hands.

'I think it's going to work!' shouted Nelly.

The rumpus inside the bedroom continued to crunch, clatter and pop until Nelly began to wonder if it would ever end.

But end it did. With crash, a bang and an unexpected medley of disco tunes, a ceasefire was suddenly called.

Nelly looked at Lump and Petal and placed her hand on the key.

Lump and Petal breathed deeply, pursed their lips tightly together and nodded.

Nelly turned the key and opened the door.

A little, at first. And then wider and wider.

They were greeted by the gummier than gummy smile of the Squurm. His tentacles had turned white with fright and his three walking sticks were snapped in two. His dentures were gone, his brighter than bright white smile had gone, but more importantly, the Tooth Furry had gone, too.

'*Yes, and I mean this most sincerely, folks, the best friend I've ever had is New Kritter-fix Plus,*' gummed the Squurm, raising a squeezed-out tube for all to admire.

'Bye bye,' said Nelly, taking the remote control from her pocket and pointing it at his forehead.

With two presses of the furry green button, the Squurm was gone, banished back to the Weirdscreen advertising break that he had been summoned from.

'I should vanish too,' thwucked Lump, 'before Petal's mum and dad come home.'

Nelly nodded and gave Lump a big hug. 'Thank you so much for coming round,' she said. 'We'll be fine now, won't we, Petal?'

Petal smiled and set about picking up her Spleeps.

'No more teeth under pillows, Nelly!' thwucked Lump, from the garden gate.

'I promise,' waved Nelly.

7

Teet and Bello returned home at quarter-past nine – very excited about the new cream-coloured Weirdscreen model they had put on order. They were a little surprised when they entered the lounge to find Nelly and Petal sitting quietly on the settee, with the Weirdscreen TV turned off.

'You're up late, Petal,' mooed Teet.

'I had a nightmare,' mooed Petal. 'Nelly said I could come down for a cuddle.'

'I hope that's OK,' said Nelly, running her fingers affectionately through Petal's udders.

'Of course it is,' mooed Teet. 'What was your nightmare about?'

'I can't remember now,' mooed Petal happily. 'Nelly made it go away.'

Nelly smiled and squeezed Petal like a tube of toothpaste.

'I must go,' she said. 'Lovely num nums, by the way.'

Teet, Bello and Petal waved Nelly goodbye from the front step.

'Lovely roses, too!' said Nelly, skipping down the path.

'You must watch our new Weirdscreen television when you come round next time, Nelly!' mooed Bello.

'I might do that!' shouted Nelly, heading for the footpath. 'Or then again, I might not,' she sighed.

Nelly was all tellied out. If she never saw another TV screen again then it wouldn't bother her in the slightest.

When she walked in through the door of her home, the house seemed eerily silent.

She went into the lounge. There was no one there. She walked into the kitchen. There was no one there.

Strange? she thought, deciding to try the garden.

'And that's just for a call-out!' groaned the pained but familiar voice of her dad. 'That's before they've even begun to unscrew the back!'

Nelly stepped through the French doors and found her dad hobbling up and down the lawn. She waved to her mum who was relaxing on a sun lounger with a glass of white wine and Asti who was sitting alongside her.

'Why's Dad limping?' Nelly whispered.

'TV repair estimate,' whispered her mum.

'You were wrong, Nelly,' said Asti, lowering her teen mag. 'I rang Natalie to see what happened in *Summerdale* and she said that Bernie Melrose didn't have a heart attack in the car on the way to the airport. Him and Dilys were actually on the plane to Majorca when they were both abducted by aliens. Apparently an alien race want Bernie's farming expertise to help them cultivate the barren red sands of another planet in a distant galaxy. How weird is that!'

Nelly parked her bum on the seat of the swing and puffed out her cheeks.

'I've seen weirder,' she smiled.

THE
PIPPLEWAKS
AT NO.66

1

'I hate that cat!' shouted Nelly, chasing down the stairs from her bedroom and charging through the kitchen into the back garden.

Nelly's mum and dad watched over the rims of their coffee cups as Nelly's whirling, swirling arms helicoptered across the lawn in pursuit of next door's black and white cat.

'Not another bird!' groaned Asti, racing into the kitchen from the lounge. 'He's always catching birds!' she cried, chasing out on to the lawn to help Nelly with the rescue mission.

Nelly's dad placed his cup on the kitchen table and sighed philosophically. 'Barney's only doing what nature intended,' he said. 'He's a cat. Cats are supposed to eat birds. It's what cats do.'

Nelly's mum watched her two daughters zigzagging around the lawn for a few moments and then entered the debate. 'It's not what next door's cat does. Barney doesn't eat the birds he catches at all. He just plays with them until they're dead,' she countered.

'As cats do,' said Nelly's dad for the defence.

'I'll tell you something else that cats do,' said Mum. 'And they do them all over our vegetable garden. And in our flower pots.'

'You're right, I hate that cat,' said Dad, charging out into the garden.

Nelly and Asti had cornered the long-haired

villain by the conifer, where it was crouched low beneath the evergreen branches, glaring up at them with cold, killer eyes.

'I think it's a sparrow,' said Asti, trying to identify the feathers that were poking out of either side of Barney's jaws.

'It's a young one,' said Nelly, spotting the custard-yellow trim on its beak.

'How do we make it drop it?' asked Asti.

'I don't know,' said Nelly, inching forwards and then back.

The trouble was, whenever one of the girls took

a step closer, the cat closed its jaws tighter. On one occasion it even growled at them.

'I didn't know cats could growl!' said Asti, for whom the cat's wickedness was fast assuming Satanic proportions.

Dad arrived and placed a consoling arm around both of his daughters' shoulders.

'The bird is dead,' he said with a shake of his head. 'Mother Nature can be cruel sometimes, girls. There's nothing we can do.'

'There's something I can do,' insisted Nelly, retrieving an aluminium bucket from the shed and a trowel from the top of Snowball's hutch.

The cat slunk low into the grass as Nelly marched up to it and then banged the bucket loudly above its head with the trowel.

The garden reverberated with a loud clang, clang, clang as the cat sprang to its feet, turned tail and scrabbled up and over the fence. Alas, with the bird still in its mouth.

'I thought it might have dropped it,' sighed Nelly. 'We could have buried it if it had dropped it.'

Nelly's dad led the girls back to the kitchen, secretly glad that the family wouldn't have to go through the rigmarole of a shoebox funeral.

'It's just nature's way,' he reminded them solemnly as they stepped on to the patio.

'Nature's way of what?' said Asti, who was in a far less forgiving mood.

Nelly's dad refixed his sights on his coffee cup and then dithered by the kitchen door.

'Er . . . cats are nature's way of, er . . . keeping the bird population, er . . . at the right level,' said Dad, who was beginning to run out of expertise in matters both feline and feathered.

'Rubbish,' said Nelly. 'There aren't enough sparrows in the world as it is; in fact, bird populations have been on the decline for years. Especially song birds. The French keep eating them and the Belgians and the Maltese keep shooting them . . .'

'The farmers keep poisoning them,' added Asti, who had read the same magazine article as Nelly.

'And that rotten cat from next door keeps catching them,' said Nelly. 'That's the third bird I've seen it catch in the last week!'

Nelly's dad decided to bow out of this particular discussion. His daughters could be formidable opposition on the rare occasions that they teamed up.

'Breakfast!' he proposed cheerfully. 'Come and join Mum and me for breakfast!'

'I'm not hungry,' said Asti, trudging through the kitchen and back to the lounge.

'Me neither,' said Nelly, returning to her bedroom to complete her latest entry in her monster-sitting diary.

'How could you possibly eat anything after watching that!' shouted Nelly from the stairs.

'Cat lover!' shouted Asti.

Nelly's dad limped to the breakfast table and stared disconsolately at his muesli. He dipped his finger into his coffee cup and shivered.

'I hate that cat,' he grumbled.

'Me too,' sighed Mum.

2

Nelly sat down by her bedroom window and picked up her purple gel pen. With a sigh of feathered bereavement, she added the letters ***KS AT NUMBER 66*** to the top of a new page in her secret monster-sitting notebook, finally completing the entry she had begun earlier.

By the time she had rendered the 66 and double underlined the whole title in silver she had begun to feel much better. She had an appointment to monster sit again that afternoon, for the Pipplewaks at Number 66 Humbug Crescent.

She had monster sat for the Sherbet Street Pipplewaks before but Humbug Crescent would be a first. Nelly liked firsts. There was something rather exciting about the unknown. She replaced the lid on her gel pen and then flicked fondly through the pages of her notebook. A smile spread across her face as adventure after adventure unfolded in her mind.

'I hope the Humbug Crescent Pipplewaks don't have triplets too,' she laughed, concealing her notebook inside the hot-water bottle and sliding it back into her secret drawer.

She didn't have to be at the Pipplewaks' house until two that afternoon and so there was plenty of time to get changed into her monster-sitting gear. Actually, it was a good job she had a few hours to kill because her sardine sweatshirt was still in the ironing basket. Knowing her mum, it was likely to remain there for some time. Nelly's mum disliked ironing as much as she disliked eating meat. In fact, if there was the ironing equivalent of a vegetarian, Nelly's mum was it.

When Nelly returned downstairs she did so *half ready* to monster sit, with her red trainers double knotted, her green jeans fastened and her long, liquorice-black hair groomed and tied back scrunchee-style.

When she walked into the kitchen, she found her mum at the sink, peeling potatoes.

'I need Sardiney for this afternoon, please Mum,' asked Nelly, prising her favourite sardine sweatshirt from the middle storey of a towering skyscraper of laundry that had banked up on the kitchen counter.

Nelly's mum paused in mid-scrape, turned palely towards the ironing basket and shuddered.

The potato peel dangled lifelessly from the potato as she blinked blankly into space. It was as though an invisible wall had formed between her and the ironing basket, actually preventing her from connecting with the laundry in any way.

Nelly raised her sardine sweatshirt in front of her mum's eyes, and then moved it slowly from left to right, like a doctor might move his finger, checking for double vision.

A low, grizzly-bear growl began to sound from deep within Nelly's mum's being. Nelly stepped back cautiously as the laundry spell suddenly broke with the splash and clatter of the potato peeler and a loud 'CLIFFORD!'

The soft-soled sound of limping slippers drew Nelly's attention to the door as her dad sheepishly poked his head into the kitchen, and smiled warily at his wife.

'Yes, Yvonne sweety?' he wavered.

'I've got ironing up to here and potato peelings up to here! Take your pick,' she boomed, retrieving the peeler from the sink and brandishing it at her husband like a flick-knife.

Nelly's dad looked at the sardine sweatshirt that Nelly had in her hands and then stared in horror at the pile of ironing that threatened to come with it.

'Potatoes,' he whimpered, shuffling across to the sink and disarming his wife.

'I'm going to need to have at least two more coffees before I can even think about your sweatshirt, Nelly,' said Nelly's mum, looking daggers at the steam iron.

'I'll come back later,' said Nelly, retreating diplomatically to the lounge.

The friendly alliance that Asti and Nelly had formed earlier dissolved the instant Nelly sat down on the settee.

'Who said you could wear my T-shirt?' said Asti, pinching her face into a fair impression of a squeezed lemon.

Nelly glanced down at her chest and shrugged.

'I'm not wearing it, I'm borrowing it,' she explained. 'Mum hasn't done any ironing for about the last seven years and I haven't got anything else to wear.'

Asti bristled and then folded her arms indignantly.

'Well, don't think for one moment that you're wearing one of my T-shirts to baby sit one of those Poppleplop freako things. I've seen your Post-it on the hallway mirror, I know where you're going this afternoon and you're not going anywhere wearing one of my T-shirts.'

'Pipplewaks not Poppleplops,' said Nelly wearily.

'I don't care what they're called,' said Asti. 'You're not getting slug slime all over my T-shirt. Muuuummmm . . . !' she whined in her familiar, wounded Asti voice.

'Don't go there,' said Nelly. 'Mum's ironing.'

Asti slunk back into her chair and winced.

'And for your information, Pipplewaks aren't slimy at all. They're feathery,' said Nelly.

'Well, for your information,' countered Asti, 'you're not borrowing my T-shirt.'

'Well, for your information,' said Nelly, 'I wouldn't want to take one of your scummy T-shirts monster sitting, even if it was the last T-shirt on earth. In fact,' she continued, 'I wouldn't even use one of your T-shirts to wipe a Grerk's bottom.'

'Good,' huffed Asti, 'because from now on, you're not allowed to borrow one thing of mine ever again.'

'Am,' said Nelly.

'Aren't,' said Asti.

'Am,' said Nelly.

'Aren't,' said Asti.

'Am,' said Nelly.

'Aren't,' said Asti . . .

Three hundred and seventy-nine 'Ams' later, Nelly's mum appeared in the lounge with Nelly's sardine sweatshirt, patchily ironed down both sleeves, but passably pressed in most other areas.

'That sardine transfer is so tricky to iron around, Nelly, please don't buy any more sweatshirts like this,' she puffed.

Nelly took hold of her sweatshirt and held it up for an inspection.

'You should turn it inside out,' she said, 'then you can run the iron straight across the transfer from the other side.'

Nelly's mum frowned.

'No, my girl – YOU should turn it inside out and YOU should run the iron across from the other side. In fact, from now on, Petronella Morton, perhaps you'd like to do your own ironing.'

Nelly groaned and flopped back into her chair.

'Aren't,' whispered Asti in triumph.

3

When Nelly left her house later that afternoon, her mum was still huffing and puffing over the ironing board in the kitchen. She had the broken look of a plantation slave.

'AM!' shouted Nelly to her sister, before slamming the front door behind her.

'AREN'T!' hollered Asti from the upstairs bedroom window as Nelly prepared to cross Sweet Street and set off north towards Humbug Crescent.

How childish, thought Nelly, skipping through a gap in the Saturday afternoon traffic. The trouble with Asti, is she never knows when to stop.

Nelly turned and looked up at her mum and dad's bedroom window from the other side of the street. She wasn't in the slightest bit surprised to see Asti, still leaning out and glaring at her.

'AM! AM! AM!' Nelly shouted back defiantly, placing both hands over her ears and running away before Asti could respond.

She was the full length of Coconut Street and halfway along Fondant Way before she removed her five-fingered earplugs and placed them back into her pockets.

'Am,' she whispered under her breath, just in case Asti had been SOOO childish as to come back at her with an out-of-earshot 'Aren't'.

It was a couple of years ago now that a new development of bungalows had been built at the northern end of the Montelimar Estate. Humbug Crescent was slap bang in the middle. Nelly knew exactly where Number 66 was, because she and her friends had been chased off the plot of Number 64 when the Crescent was a building site. The thunder-faced foreman chasing them at the time had fortunately tripped over a bag of plaster and toppled headlong into a pile of sharp sand, allowing Nelly and her friends to make a laughter-filled escape. Even now, though, long after the homes had been built and moved into, Nelly half expected the foreman to reappear, waving a rough-knuckled fist and threatening to bury her in some wet cement foundations.

She paused to cross Allsorts Avenue, dashed furtively past Sherbet Street and scampered quickly into Blackjack Street. There was no need for alarm. The coast was clear. There was no sign of the foreman anywhere and the Humbug homes were fast approaching. Nelly turned into the Crescent and began to admire the transformation. There were no piles of bricks to hurtle around, no piles of sand to hurdle and no angry builders to evade; just evenly-laid, grey slabbed pavements, rows of low-slung bungalow roofs and a patchwork of tarmac drives and lawns.

Nelly stopped still for a moment outside Number 66 and stared quizzically at the Pipplewaks' garden gate. It reminded her of the door to a budgie cage. It had a wire-framed aluminium look and feel to it, and a simple hook latch that you could prise open with your thumb. It opened outwards with a lightweight squeak and rested with a lopsided slant against a newly-planted laurel hedge.

'Typical Pipplewak,' smiled Nelly, walking down the path and trying to smooth away an all-too-conspicuous crease that her mum had ironed into her sweatshirt. She stopped at the step. There was no doorbell to ring, only a heavy brass knocker to ratatat.

Nelly looked at her watch. She was three seconds early. With an extra tat for luck, she stepped excitedly back from the step and waited for the Pipplewaks to answer.

The door flew open almost the moment she had released the knocker.

'Come in, Nelly! Please come in!' trilled a puff-chested Pipplewak, beckoning her inside with four friendly wings. The fringe of Nelly's hair lifted upwards slightly as the up-draught from the Pipplewak's feathers gently fanned her face.

'I can't tell you what a pleasure it is to meet

'Come on, Nelly! Please come in!'

you, Nelly!' he trilled, turning with a hop and bouncing like a crow down the hall. 'Our cousins in Sherbet Street were ever so complimentary about you!'

Nelly stepped inside and wiped her feet with a rasp. (Pipplewaks have sandpaper doormats and carpets.)

'It's a pleasure to meet you too!' laughed Nelly, closing the door quickly and hurrying to keep up with a long, kangaroo-like tail as it looped along the hallway. 'By the way, you haven't told me your name!'

As the tip of the Pipplewak's tail trailed around the corner, Nelly braced herself for a formal introduction. Ironing her sweatshirt quickly with the flats of her hands, she composed herself and entered the lounge.

'This is my wife Millet,' trilled a blue beak.

'And this is my husband Bill,' trilled a white beak.

The Pipplewak couple were standing side by side in the middle of a large, open-plan room, smiling broadly with giant, nut-cracking beaks. Nelly's eyes craned upwards into the high-vaulted ceiling space and then down at her hosts. They looked like newly-weds. They had four wings wrapped around each other in a warm embrace and the distinct look of love birds about them. Love birds of the African Plains variety, that is, for the build of each Pipplewak was far more akin to an ostrich than a turtledove. They had stout, feathered chests of strikingly bright purple plumage and white ostrich legs that sported gnarled and knobbly knees. Their orange feet pressed flat to the floor like five-pointed starfish with a single toenail that hooked sharply like a sloth claw.

Of course Nelly had seen it all before, having monster sat for their Sherbet Street cousins some months ago. The Humbug Crescent couple were almost identical in every way. The only difference, as far as Nelly could make out, was the incredible sparkle in their eyes. Both sets of three were dangling and dancing from their stalks like twinkling blue fibre optics. Happiness was definitely in the air.

Nelly stepped forward confidently and held out her hand. As she did so, the Pipplewaks curtsied low and then parted like theatre curtains.

'It's lovely to be he . . . . . . re,' faltered Nelly, dropping her eyes into the space that had opened up between the two Pipplewaks. For there on the floor, directly behind them, nestled snugly in a nest of pink loft insulation, was an egg. A huge lemon-coloured egg, the size and circumference of a loo seat.

Nelly gawped for a moment and then waited mutely for the right words to come. But they wouldn't. Her vocabulary had completely deserted her. And no wonder! Not only was the biggest egg she had ever seen sitting in the middle of the lounge, it was wearing headphones.

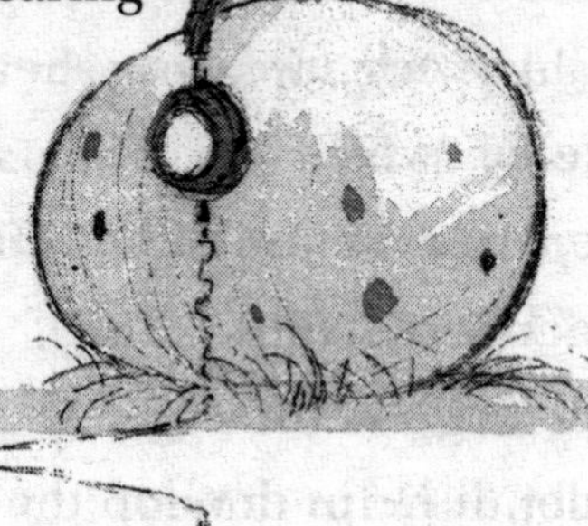

'An egg!' gasped Nelly, managing a couple of words at last.

'Our egg,' trilled Millet and Bill proudly.

'A big egg,' gasped Nelly, who was fast becoming a contender for the Nobel Obviousness Prize.

'Thank you,' trilled Millet. 'Are you surprised?'

'Yes, I mean no, I mean I'm not sure really,' said Nelly. 'I'm never sure what to expect when I go monster sitting,' she blustered.

Millet and Bill beckoned Nelly forward with a brace of friendly flaps. Nelly took two uncertain steps towards the nest and then ran her eyes along the headphone lead that coiled like a num num across the sandpaper floor to a plug socket located on the far wall.

'An egg, wearing headphones?' mumbled Nelly, who was still struggling to regain constructive use of her tongue.

'That's right, Nelly,' trilled Bill, looking adoringly at the egg. 'We're playing music to our baby. It helps develop the mind at an early age.'

'Do humans do that too, Nelly?' trilled Millet.

Nelly shook herself out of gaga mode and tried to engage her brain.

'Er . . . actually er . . . yes, I have heard of people doing that before,' she blustered. 'Forgive me,' Nelly said. 'I've never seen er . . . headphones that big before,' she continued, not wanting to be rude about the size of the egg.

'They're just normal-sized headphones,' trilled Bill, stroking the egg lovingly with the tips of his wings.

Nelly knelt low, bringing her head to egg height. Encouraged by the smiles of the Pipplewak parents-to-be, she reached out with her fingers and ran them softly over the contours of the lemon shell. It felt smooth, warm and strong, like a sun-baked beach pebble.

'May I?' she asked politely.

'Be our guest,' smiled Millet.

Nelly leant forward and placed her ear delicately against the shell, listening intently for sounds of life. But she could hear nothing above the soft, tinny tink of the music emitting from the headphones.

'Have you decided on a name?' she asked.

'Grozzle if it's a boy,' trilled Millet.

'Mush if it's a girl,' trilled Bill.

Nelly nodded uncertainly and decided not to enquire about middle names.

'How unusual,' she said, standing back up to rub the sandpaper grains from the knees of her jeans. 'Now then, it's time you introduced me to your other children!'

Millet turned her beak towards her husband.

'There are no other children, Nelly,' trilled Bill. 'We want you to look after our egg.'

Nelly stood stunned for a moment. She twitched her nose, swallowed dryly and then gave the Pipplewaks a resoundingly positive double thumbs-up.

'Of course you do!' she smiled. 'Of course you want me to monster sit your egg. I knew that all along. I'd be delighted to monster sit your egg!'

'It shouldn't be any trouble, Nelly,' trilled

Millet. 'It's not due to hatch until next Thursday.'

'That's good!' said Nelly, smiling a little apprehensively at the nest.

'If it's all right with you, Nelly, we'd like to take a short trip to the hardware store to see if we can buy some of those new ultra-absorbent sandpaper sheets for the cot,' said Millet. 'Have you seen them advertised on the telly?'

Nelly shook her head. She had avoided monster TV channels since her visit to the Cowcumbers at Parma Drive.

'Pipplewak babies can be very messy,' trilled Bill. 'Quadruple-ply sandsheets with triple-absorbency action are just what we'll need for the cot!'

Nelly followed the flap of Millet's wings across the open-plan floor. A steel-framed cot with prison-strength bars had been given pride of place by the French windows.

'Really?' gulped Nelly, who was secretly beginning to grow a little anxious at even the slimmest chance of becoming an emergency midwife. If Pipplewaks were messy when they were babies you could bet your life they were even messier when they were being born. Nelly had watched birth films in Personal Development lessons at school. She knew how messy 'messy' could be.

'We'll only be gone a couple of hours,' trilled Bill. 'If it's a problem, we'll happily stay here at home.'

Nelly shook her head bullishly and then waved the expectant parents towards the door.

'You go ahead,' she smiled. 'I'll be perfectly fine with a Grozzle or a Mush! Or hopefully an egg still!'

Millet and Bill were reassured by Nelly's show of confidence and allowed themselves to be shepherded out of the lounge and ushered towards the front door. But as Millet hopped out on to the front step, she felt compelled to put Nelly further at ease. She turned with a flap and a swish of her tail and placed two wings on each of Nelly's shoulders.

'*If* the egg *does* hatch, Nelly . . .'

'And *we're sure it won't*,' trilled Bill, with an emphatic shake of his beak.

'But *if, if, if* the egg hatches *and we're, sure, sure sure that it won't*,' trilled Millet, 'here are some instructions. Just do as this says, and you'll be fine . . .'

Nelly waited in the doorway as Millet opened her clutchbag and carefully put pen to paper. It was a short note which she folded once with each wing and then handed to Nelly for safekeeping. Nelly tucked it into the back pocket of her jeans and then stepped back as Millet hopped back into the bungalow and bounced two-footed down the hallway.

'I won't be a moment,' she trilled, 'there's just one more thing I need to do, just in case.'

Nelly turned to Bill and smiled. 'I'll be fine,' she laughed. 'As you say, the egg isn't due to hatch for at least five days yet, is it?'

'Exactly, Nelly! Next Thursday. Pipplewaks eggs *never* hatch early,' trilled Bill. 'Well, hardly ever.'

'He's right, Nelly,' trilled Millet, returning from the kitchen, job done. 'Our egg really shouldn't hatch . . . We promise.'

Nelly nodded appreciatively. She liked the word *promise* and was particularly encouraged by the word *never.* But when she closed the front door of the bungalow, she looked at her watch and nibbled her lip. For, somehow, she couldn't help thinking that feathers were going to fly.

4

Nelly walked back into the living area and stared at the egg. True to the Pipplewaks' word, it was as motionless as a boulder screwed to a floor. 'Ho hum,' sighed Nelly, turning her attention to the room.

Usually when she monster sat and the parents had just left, the place erupted with excitement. But in the absence of any children there was a strange emptiness. The open-plan layout of the building made the house feel emptier still.

As is always the way with a Pipplewak's home there was a distinctive bird theme to the furnishings.

'I should have brought my cozzie!' she smiled, ambling over to one end of the room and peering into the spa-sized depths of a circular, white marble bird bath. It was big enough to take three emus at once and had four Jacuzzi jet modes. Nelly strummed her fingers idly across the buttons and then strolled casually to the other end of the room towards the nursery zone.

Adjacent to the cot, Nelly found the Pipplewaks' kitchen area. It was ever so slightly annexed by a waist-height partition wall. Nelly threw a glance inside but didn't need to enter to see that there was no washing-up that needed doing or potatoes that needed peeling. Not that Nelly was a big fan of tea towels or peelers, but at least it would have been something to do.

Four paces to her left she found a book on a shelf. *My First Pipplewak Alphabet Picture Book* lay within wing's reach of the bars. ***D*** is for **D**inner, the open page read.

'And ***D***on'tknowwhattodo,' sighed Nelly.

She replaced the book on the shelf and turned to a mobile, suspended from the ceiling above the cot. The abstract tubular shapes jangled like wind chimes as she ran her fingers through them, throwing afternoon shadows across the wall.

Nelly watched with dreamy detachment for a moment and then refocused on the room.

Just like Sherbet Street, there were no settees or armchairs to sit on. Instead, there were polished wooden trapeze bars suspended by sturdy chains from the ceiling. Pipplewaks much preferred to perch than to sit.

Nelly ambled past the fireplace and perched her own bottom down on a two-seater. She felt like she was on a garden swing, without the trees, the leaves and the lawn.

Stifling a yawn, she returned her gaze to the egg, nestling in the nest in the middle of the floor. It was enormous. In fact, if it had been chocolate it would have taken her all four days of Easter to eat it.

'I wonder if it unscrews like a Veri egg or cracks like a chicken egg?' she mused, kicking a little harder with her feet and swaying back and forth with a little more oomph.

She applied the brakes with the soles of her

trainers and jumped down from the perch. She could see another, smaller chain hanging from the ceiling in the corner of the room, with a polished chrome object attached.

Nelly went to investigate. In profile it looked like a Christmas decoration, but from the front it revealed itself to be a giant budgie mirror.

'Hello, me,' smiled Nelly to herself.

'Hello, you,' replied her reflection.

'How am I today?'

'I'm fine, thanks.'

'Me too. I'm monster sitting for the Pipplewaks.'

'Me too!'

'Actually, I'm monster sitting an egg.'

'Me too!'

'What a coincidence.'

'I can say that again!'

Nelly leant forward and examined her teeth and then stepped back to peer at her sweatshirt. It wasn't exactly a life-changing moment, but for the first time in her life she realised that *sardine* spelt *enibras* backwards. Well, sort of.

She pushed the mirror playfully and then turned again to the egg. It did look strange, sitting in the middle of the floor wearing headphones.

'It's time I introduced myself,' Nelly said, walking across to the nest and sitting cross-legged on the floor beside it.

'Hello, Egg,' she said. 'My name's Nelly the Monster Sitter. I'm very pleased to meet you.'

The egg sat in its nest and did what eggs do. Precisely nothing.

'Are you looking forward to the big day?' continued Nelly. 'Only five days to go now, before you become a Grozzle or a Mush. Exciting, eh?'

If the egg was excited, it certainly wasn't letting on. Nelly leant forward a little to examine the shell. There was no visible join in the middle like a Veri egg, and no hinges or other clues as to how the egg might open next Thursday.

'What sort of music are you listening to?' whispered Nelly, trying to decipher the tink, tink, tink of the headphones. She craned her neck forward and angled her ear closer to the headphone on the right side of the egg.

'Let me guess. Something by the Beakles!' she smiled.

The egg nestled humourlessly before her.

'Do you think I could have a listen?' asked Nelly inquisitively, ping-ponging her eyes from one headphone to the other. 'I'm sure it would be all right if I had a little listen, wouldn't it?'

There were no nods of approval from the egg – but equally, there were no shakes of disapproval, either. Nelly took that as a yes.

Shuffling forward on her bottom, she placed both hands around the headphones and gently eased them upwards. The headphones closed like crabs claws, before sliding off, springing shut and falling into Nelly's lap.

'You can have them back in a minute,' said Nelly, raising the headphones with both hands but struggling to prise them open again. They were much stiffer to reopen than Nelly had imagined. She grunted and groaned, heaved the headphones ten centimetres apart and then gasped as they sprang shut again and dropped back into her lap.

'Maybe I won't put them on, maybe I'll just hold them to my ear,' she reasoned, swivelling one of the earphones one hundred and eighty degrees and pressing it to the side of her face.

Nelly listened hard. And no wonder. It was hard music to listen to. The best way she could describe it was 'rock bird song', a warbling chirrup of hedgerow sounds mixed with electric guitar. There was possibly a seagull in there somewhere and perhaps some wood block and maracas too. Nelly thought of another way to describe it. Row without the hedge.

'You can have them back now,' she shuddered.

She picked up the headphones and tried to prise them apart again. But it was like trying to open a rusty nutcracker.

Her cheeks flushed red and her teeth began to grind.

'Open up!' she grimaced, tensing her biceps to breaking point.

Her elbows had begun to wobble, and her dimples began to twitch.

She was winning. She was definitely winning. The headphones were definitely parting.

Nelly furrowed her brow and growled like a Huffaluk.

'Opennnnnn!' she groaned.

The headphones slowly began to open but she still had to slip them gently into position over the egg.

The vein in her temple had begun to stick out and her jugular had begun to bulge, but she was definitely getting there.

She inched them over the apex of the egg and

prepared to clamp them softly into place.

'Gently,' she grimaced. 'Gently,' she groaned. Her arms began to tremble under the strain and her eyes began to water.

'Nearly there,' she squeaked, lowering the headphones gently, gently, gently over the shell, in readiness to ease them softly into position.

'Nearly there . . . nearly there—' RATATATAT-ATAT!

Nelly jumped like a flea as the Pipplewaks' door knocker rattled like a machine-gun through the echoey emptiness of the room.

Her composure shattered, her wrists buckled and the headphones snapped like a bear trap on to the shell of the egg.

Nelly screamed a silent scream and looked in horror at the shell. There was a crack.

There was a definite crack running right around the middle of the egg!

'Aaaaargghhh!' she gasped, placing both hands over her mouth and then wheeling her head in the direction of the hallway. A minefield of uncertainties began to detonate in her mind.

Who was at the door? Was it the Pipplewaks? If it was the Pipplewaks, surely they would have a key? Why had they knocked so loudly? It must be important. Maybe it was urgent! She looked at the egg. She stared at the crack. Was it going to hatch? Wasn't it going to hatch? Maybe it wasn't a crack as such. Perhaps it was more *hairline* than *crack*. After all, it hadn't grown in the last nanosecond. Maybe it wouldn't grow any more!

Nelly sprang to her feet in a blind panic, raced down the hall and wrenched open the front door.

There was no one there! Confusion avalanched through her brain.

She looked down the path, she stared left, she peered right. There was absolutely no one at the door at all. Her heart began to tom-tom. What was going on? She was sure someone had knocked on the door. But who? And where had they gone?

She stood for a moment with leaden legs and then dropped her gaze to her feet.

There, lying on the doorstep before her, was an envelope. A plain white envelope addressed in blue Biro to 'NELLY'.

Nelly snatched it up and tore it open. There was a single piece of blue notepaper inside, bearing the one word message:

'AREN'T!'

Nelly stared at the message for a millibeat and then sprang her eyes in the direction of Blackjack Street. She was just in time to see the familiar orange cardigan of her sister hurtling round the corner out of sight.

'AAASTI!' she screamed, tearing the note into confetti and hurling it at the floor. 'It's all your fault!'

5

A living, breathing, twelve-kilo, oven-ready turkey, with four flapping, featherless wings and a beak of industrial proportions. That was one way of describing the Pipplewak chick that had hatched during Nelly's momentary absence. A nightmare with no feathers was another.

Nelly sat motionless on her knees and stared dumbstruck into the bottom segment of the eggshell. A wet, glistening Pipplewak chick was sitting in an oily stew of egg white and snot, struggling to heave itself out of its shell. With every flap of its bald, bony wings it was basting itself and the carpet with goo.

Nelly closed her eyes and grimaced as she was splatted across both cheeks.

'PEEP!' squawked the chick, with a loud, bullfroggish rasp.

Nelly's own response was less vocal. Words had deserted her for the second time that day. All she could do was kneel and stare.

'PEEEP!' rasped the Pipplewak chick again, turning its scrawny, sausage-skin neck towards Nelly and fixing her with three dingling-dangling blue eyes.

Nelly's eyes widened in horror as the chick

suddenly rose from the stew on thin, feeble legs and toppled sideways out of the egg. The shell overturned like an upside-down saucepan, sending thin viscous goo flooding across the carpet towards Nelly's knees.

Nelly sprang up and then jumped forward, saving the headphones from flood damage and trailing them back towards the wall.

'PEEEEP!' foghorned the chick again, craning its neck upwards and trying to untangle five starfish toes and a kangaroo tail from behind its back.

Nelly put her hands over her ears and winced.

'PEEEEEP!' it thundered again.

'It wants me to pick it up!' gasped Nelly. 'I hope it doesn't think I'm its mum.'

Nelly had heard strange stories before about ducklings adopting the first thing they see as their mother.

'PEEEEEEEP!' rasped the big booming beak again.

'It *definitely* wants me to pick it up,' shuddered Nelly.

She was right. The newly-born Pipplewak chick was teetering on the lip of the nest, staring intently in Nelly's direction. Its featherless sausage-skin body was glistening with oily goo and its pink chipolata wings were fluttering manically.

Nelly gulped hard. She was kind of hoping that some motherly instincts might kick in fast, but if she felt protective towards anything, it was her sardine sweatshirt. She really did not want to get Pipplewak birth fluids all over her favourite monster-sitting sweatshirt. She looked around the room for some post-natal-favourite-sweatshirt-protection-vests, but wasn't entirely surprised to be disappointed.

'PEEEE*EEPP*!' squawked the Pipplewak chick, suddenly tumbling off the lip of the nest and squelching headlong on to the sandpaper carpet.

Nelly ran instinctively across the carpet, forgot about her sweatshirt, heaved the chick off the floor and cradled the big oily lump in her arms. It weighed a ton. A bouncing twelve kilos, eight grammes, to be precise.

'*PEEEEEEEEP PEEEEP!*' thundered the chick, five centimetres from Nelly's ear.

Nelly shuddered and her brain jangled. 'Keep the noise down!' she gasped, running inquisitive eyes over the chick at close quarters. There was no sign of a volume control. There were signs of feathers, though. Close up, she could see that the chick's pink, oily skin was peppered with little purple bobbles, all of them feathers in the making.

'You're quite cute actually, aren't you,' she said, heaving the chick like a sack of potatoes into a more comfortable cradle position and tickling one of its orange claws with a finger.

'*PEEEEEEEEEEEEEEEEEEEEP!*' exploded the chick.

Nelly's eyes crossed and her head shook as she tried to absorb the decibels.

'What does PEEP mean?' she shuddered.

The chick's wings began to vibrate again with frenzied, trembling flaps.

Nelly looked at the nest and then over towards

the cot. Her arms were aching already and she needed somewhere to put the chick down. The cot seemed the best place, sandsheets or no sandsheets. It was birth-fluid free, it had the advantage of being clean and dry and the added bonus of having steel bars to stop the chick from tumbling out.

'Come and meet your cot,' said Nelly, staggering across the floor with an armful of beak cradled to her chest. 'Actually, wait here for a moment,' she said, lowering the chick to the floor adjacent to the cot. 'I'm just going to get you a sandsheet to poop on.'

The chick wobbled unsteadily on cocktail-stick-thin legs as Nelly raced to the front door and returned with the doormat under her arm.

'This will have to do for now,' she said, using it to line the base of the cot.

The Pipplewak chick PPPPEEEEEEEEEEEEEEPed again as Nelly lifted it up and heaved it over the bars with a groan.

Without thinking, she wiped her fingers on her

jeans, and then groaned at the sight of the transfer on her sweatshirt. *Sardine* was now *sardine in oil.*

'Mum'll kill me,' she groaned, trying her best to wipe it clean with her sleeve.

She wiped her brow with her other sleeve and then jumped back in astonishment as the Pipplewak chick lurched towards the end of the cot and pressed its beak and wings through the bars.

'PEEEEEEEEEEEEEEEEEEEEEPPPPPPPPPPPPPP!' thundered the heavy-duty beak. It was pointing excitedly at the kitchen.

The chick wanted something and it wanted it bad. Nelly stood, puzzled for a moment, and then plunged her fingers into the back pocket of her jeans. She had suddenly remembered the note that Millet had handed her before leaving with Bill.

She unravelled it fast and zeroed in on the instructions.

In soft, feathery writing they read: *If egg*

hatches, please feed . . . (Food in kitchen.)

Nelly stared at the note and stared at the chick. Its beak was about to open again. She cupped her hands over her ears quickly and rocked in her socks as another cavernous 'PEEEEEEEEEEEE-EEEEEEEEEEEEEEEEEEEEEEEEEEEEEP!' shook the room.

'You're hungry!' she smiled. 'That's what you're telling me. You're hungry!'

Quickly folding the note and placing it back into her pocket, she dashed into the kitchen area.

'Aha!' she laughed, spotting a small, yellow Post-it note, stuck at low level on the fridge door.

The word *Food* had been added in Millet's handwriting.

Nelly glanced at the cooker. An identical Post-it had been slapped on to the cooker door, too.

'Now we're in business!' said Nelly confidently. 'We'll have ample provisions here!' She smiled at the chick and skipped over to the fridge.

'What's it going to be?' she said, opening the fridge door and peering inside.

The chick's scrawny, sausage-skin neck stretched like a Christmas stocking through a gap in the bars and its huge, earth-moving jaws craned open wide.

Nelly reached inside the fridge to the top shelf. It was empty.

She darted her hand downwards to the shelf below. It was empty too.

So was the next shelf down.

Nelly dropped to her knees and put her head into the fridge space. It was empty, empty, empty, empty. There wasn't even a fridge light and it didn't even feel cold.

'PPPPPPPEEEEEEEEEEEEEEEEEEEEEEEEEEEEEE-PPPPPPPPPPPPPPPPPP!' echoed the cavernous jaws of the Pipplewak chick, as Nelly stood up and closed the fridge door. Nelly placed both hands on the top of the fridge and peered down the back. It didn't even have a plug.

She turned to the chick. It was blue in the face and crimson in the beak. Its pupils were burning emerald green and its dingle-dangle eye-stalks were now as rigid as pencils. Its stomach was gurgling, too. With a flurry of featherless wings and an impatient stamp of its ten orange toes, it pointed to the fridge again.

Nelly tried the cooker instead. More in hope than in expectation, for if Millet hadn't had time to stock the fridge before leaving, it was doubtful that she had had time to prepare a cooked meal.

The sandsheet doormat began to rasp like an electric sander beneath the Pipplewak chick's feet as its excited stamping turned to a sand dance. Nelly opened the cooker door and bent down to peer inside. Contrary to the Post-it note label, there was no food whatsoever inside the cooker, either. The shelves certainly showed evidence of recent cooking activity, in fact if Nelly wasn't mistaken there was a familiar whiff of burnt Yorkshire pudding lurking at the back of the top shelf.

But there was no baby food. No rusks, no milk, no gripe water, no jars of vegetable bake or cottage pie or even mushed Lumpet and Weeps or whatever it was that monster babies ate. There was nothing in either the cooker, the fridge, or the kitchen cupboards for that matter. The Pipplewaks' kitchen was agonisingly bare.

'PPPPPPPPPPPPPPPPPEEEEEEEEEEEEEEEEEEEEEEEEEE-EEEEEEEEEEEEEPPPPPPPPPPPPPPPPPPPPPP-PPPPPPPPPPPP!' protested the chick as Nelly closed the oven door and scratched her head. There had to be some food for the baby Pipplewak, or at least some food of some kind, somewhere. But where?

There was a door. A door leading from the kitchen to the garage. Maybe there was a chest freezer unit out there, full of baby food. After all, that's where Nelly's mum and dad kept their frozen grub at home. Nelly dived for the handle, turned the key and threw the door open. (As far as she could.)

The door reverberated with a crack and a judder as it swung back and collided with something hard. Nelly groaned. The garage was crammed full with junk. Old cookers, old fridges, car parts, hub caps, hi-fi systems and microwaves were piled high from floor to ceiling. It was more like a salvage yard than a garage.

'Now what am I going to do?' she groaned, wishing she had another Post-it note to instruct her. She hurried back to the cot and tried her best to calm the chick down. But this beak wasn't for comforting. It was for eating. This monster chick was beside itself with hunger. Its eyes were bulging, its stomach was gurgling and its wings were flapping like palm leaves in a hurricane.

'But there's no food in the house!' sighed Nelly. 'I've looked!'

A new kind of PEEP began to issue from the chick. It exchanged 'e's for 'o's and was beginning to issue with an ominous grumble from the opposite end of its body.

'POOOOOOOOOOOOOOOOOOOOOOOOOO-OOOOOOOOOOP!' growled the chick's bottom. SQUELCH went the cot mat.

Nelly waved the steam from her face, took a tentative step forward and peered gingerly into the base of the cot. In the beak-bursting frustration of the moment, the chick had opened its undercarriage and the cot was now awash with yellow gloop. Tiny suckers sprang immediately from its orange starfish feet as the baby chick began to slip and slide.

'Gross,' shuddered Nelly, instantly changing her plan to comfort the chick with a cuddle and instead trying to stroke a gloop-free part of its body through the bars.

'There, there,' she soothed. 'Mummy and Daddy will be home soon.'

But this chick wasn't for soothing, either. It was hopping up and down like a kangaroo now, lashing its tail and snapping its beak upwards at the cot mobile. Nelly stood far enough back not to be splashed with gloop and tried to interpret the chick's sudden obsession with the metal tubes suspended above its head.

'Worms!' she gasped. 'You're trying to tell me you like worms! I'll dig you some up!'

Certain that the chick would be safe inside the

cot, Nelly decided to venture into the back garden for a moment to see if she could dig up some baby-bird sustenance with a garden spade. Assuming the Pipplewaks had a garden spade, that was.

They didn't. Neither did they have a garden in the truest sense of the word. When Nelly levered open the back door and stepped outside into the afternoon sunshine, she found not a lawn or a patio, but Tarmac, nothing but Tarmac stretching in a straight line from the French doors right down to the back fence.

The Sherbet Street Pipplewaks' back garden had been the same.

Another loud PEEEP refocused her thoughts.

'Worms!' she gasped.

But as is often the way with a soil-free garden, there were zilcho worms to be found. To Nelly's frustration, she returned back indoors with nothing more than two dead ladybirds and a greenfly.

'PPPPPPPPPPPPPEEEEEEEEEEEEEEEEE-

EEEEEEEEEEEEEEEEEEEEEEEEEEEEEEEEEE-EEEEEEEEEEEEEEEEEEEEEEEEEEEEEEEEEE-EEEEEEEEEEEEEEEEEEEEEEEEEEEEEEEEEP!' squawked the chick, apoplectic with rage and frustration.

Nelly held out her meagre, wormless offering and then jumped again as the chick began to hurl itself in frustration at the bars of the cot.

'Time for drastic action,' Nelly murmured, stuffing her hand into her pocket and prising her mobile phone from her jeans.

'I'll ring the Sherbet Street Pipplewaks! If anyone knows what to feed a Pipplewak, it's a Pipplewak!'

'Maybe they could bring some baby food round!'

'PPPPPPPPPPPPPPPPPPPEEEEEEEEEEEEEEE-EEEEEEEEEEEPPPPPPPPOOOOOOO OOOOOOO-OOOOOOOOOOOOOOOOOOOOOOOOOP!' erupted the chick with another squelch.

'Where's it all coming from?' sighed Nelly, peering at the warm, mustardy gloop that was trickling through the bars of the cot.

With an anxious bite of her lip, Nelly flipped open the cover of her mobile and punched out the first digit of her Pipplewak friends' telephone number. The tip of her index finger folded on impact and her shoulders sagged with dismay. She had no battery left on her phone!

She had meant to put it on charge that morning but had been distracted by that rotten black and white cat!

Another loud 'PPPPPPPPPPPPEEEEEEEEEE-EEEEEEEEEEEEEEEEEEEEEEEEEEEEE-EEEEEEEEEEEEEEEEEEEEEEEEEEEEE-EEEEEEEEEEEEEEEEEEEEEEEEEEEEEE-EEEEEEEEEEEEEEEEEEEEEEEEEP!' shook the room to its foundations.

'No battery!' exclaimed and explained Nelly, holding her mobile phone through the cot bars in desperation to prove to the chick that no dial tone was available.

The Pipplewak chick stared tri-eyed at the phone and then took a voracious snap at Nelly's arm.

'It tried to eat ME that time!' she gasped, withdrawing her phone like a shot. 'I know what I can do!' said Nelly, determined that all was not lost. 'I can use the Pipplewaks' home phone instead!'

Nelly spun round and scoured the room. Where did the Pipplewaks keep their phone? Her eyes bounced from the kitchen to the shelf to the fireplace and over to the sill of the front window. There was nothing on the edge of the bird bath; in fact, the only thing she could see that was plugged into a wall was the lead to the headphones. There had to be a telephone in the room somewhere. If she could find the lead she could find the phone.

She rested her eyes on a trapeze bar for a moment and then followed the chains high up into the roof space of the vaulted ceiling. There, quite bizarrely, just below the apex of the roof and fixed flat to the wall was the telephone socket.

Nelly wilted. Of all the places to keep a

How on earth was she going to get up there?

telephone, the Pipplewaks kept theirs five metres out of reach!

As her eyes soared, her heart sank.

She stared up at the ceiling and traced the path of the telephone lead through the air. It looped like a tightrope wire high up above her head to a roof beam suspended horizontally between two walls. Nelly stepped back and peered up. She could see the telephone perched on the roof beam six metres up.

She shook her head and placed her hands on her hips. How on earth was she going to get up there?

6

Nelly stared, trance-like, up at the telephone. She felt like a military engineer confronted with a mountain.

'PPPPPPPPPPPPPPPPPPPPEEEEEEEEEEEEEEEEEEEEEEEEEEEEEEEEEEEEEEEEEEEEEEEEEEEEEEEEEEEEEEEEEEEEEEEEEEEEEEPPPPPP!' roared the Pipplewak chick.

Nelly snapped out of her trance and then turned apologetically in the direction of the cot. The chick was beside itself with hunger, pointing all four of its featherless wings at the cooker in the kitchen and stamping its feet in a fury.

'I know you're hungry,' said Nelly sympathetically, 'and I'm trying to find you some food. I just need to make a call!'

The chick began slapping its forehead with

alternate wings and then hopping up and down in its own gloop.

'Someone's going to need a bath tonight,' winced Nelly, turning her attention back up to the roof. 'Now, how am I going to reach that phone?' she mused. 'I've got no ladders and I'm fresh out of pole-vault poles, too.'

She stepped back, stroked her chin thoughtfully and then looked with steely determination at the trapeze bars.

'I wonder if I can swing high enough? If I can, I might be able to hook my foot around the telephone lead and drag the telephone down from the beam,' she surmised.

For someone with no circus training, it was an ambitious plan to say the least. But Nelly walked back twenty paces and eased her bottom on to a single-seater trapeze. She was determined to have a go.

With daredevil resolve, she took firm hold of the chain either side of her. With a backward thrust and a powerful kick of her legs, she set the polished wooden perch in motion. Her progress was steady at first but soon she was building momentum.

Backwards and forwards she swooped, leaning full force backwards on the upswing and full force forwards on the downswing.

With every swoop she drew nearer to the roof. With every heave she arced closer to the beam.

Her pony-tail began to loop and her cheeks began to puff as her height and momentum began to build further.

She glanced down backwards at the cot on the upswing. She had an aerial view of the Pipplewak chick and an unsightly view of the gloop.

She refocused. Her plan of reaching the telephone lead with her ankles was suddenly and surprisingly beginning to appear viable.

She was building up G-force momentum with every swing now and her stomach was beginning to churn big time.

She pursed her lips and kicked even harder, but as the trapeze bar surged, her bottom began to slip. Danger was looming now, as well as the ceiling.

She tightened her grip on the chains and fixed her sights on the beam. Even with her foot fully outstretched, the lead was still a metre from her toe.

To reach it she was going to have to find three extra gears.

She kicked again, rocketing upwards towards the ceiling and then dive-bombing backwards towards the floor.

With every swoop, her grip on the seat became more precarious. She kicked again.

And again.

With every surge of the backswing the wooden perch slid precariously past her calves. With every orbiting upward swoop her bottom slipped perilously to the lip of her seat.

She could barely hold on. She could barely look. And yet she had to hold on and she had to look. If she wanted to make those telephone calls she had to hook her foot round that lead.

She braced herself for the next pendulum swing. With superhuman bravery, she clamped her fingers tightly around the chains, gritted her teeth and leant back, parallel to the floor.

'This time,' she gasped, knowing that one more exerted push could bring success – or a high altitude fall.

With a determined glance upwards at the beam and a 'GERONIMO!' yell, she threw the full weight of her body into the upswing and propelled herself towards the ceiling.

The floor disappeared, the telephone lead loomed and Nelly's stomach turned to upside-down pudding.

She was a shoelace away. The toes inside her trainers began to stretch. Every sinew in her body began to fray.

She was centimetres away from her target. Millimetres away from a direct hit.

With a last gasp, a wiggle and a lunge, Nelly wrenched her ankle to breaking point and hooked the toe of her right trainer around the lead.

'Gotcha!' she whooped, pulling her foot back sharply on the very peak of the upswing and watching with relief as the telephone tumbled from its high-altitude shelf and began to plummet to the floor.

'Oh no!' she groaned on the downswing, as the lead tightened at full stretch, whiplashed sharply like a bungee rope and then Tarzanned sideways towards the wall.

Nelly watched, as stiff as a corpse, as the Pipplewaks' telephone crunched into the wall like a demolition ball and broke into half a dozen pieces.

'PPPPPPPPPPPPPPPEEEEEEEEEEEEEEEEE-EEEEEEEEEEEEEEEEEEEEEEEEEEEEEEEEEEE-EEEEEEEEEEEEEEEEEEEEEEEEEEEEEEEEEEE-EEPPPPPPPPPPP!' screamed the Pipplewak chick, as crumbs of plastic and technology bounced across the floor towards the cot.

Nelly didn't want to peep. She wanted to weep.

7

She sat frozen on the trapeze bar and stared into space.

Her only chance of getting the Pipplewak chick something to eat had disintegrated before her eyes. Despite her best and bravest efforts, she had failed. There was absolutely nothing more that she could do now. She and the Pipplewak chick had no choice but to wait for Millet and Bill to return home.

She loosened her grip on the chains, slackened her body and allowed the trapeze bar to swing gradually to a halt. With a half-hearted sigh, she finally applied the brake with the toe of her trainer and slipped her bottom off its perch.

The Pipplewak chick's head poked through the bars of the cot and the stalks of its eyes began to droop. It was all peeped out. Nelly shuffled miserably over to the cot and placed a consoling hand on its beak.

'I'd love to feed you, you know I would,' she sighed, 'but there isn't a scrap of food in the house. You really must wait till your mum and dad come home.'

The chick flapped its wings weakly and turned desperately towards the kitchen.

'They won't be long,' assured Nelly.

The chick looked bewildered. Not only did it seem to have lost its voice, it appeared to be losing its will to live. It wobbled unsteadily on its feet, shook its beak groggily and then toppled backwards on to the gloop-covered sandsheet.

Nelly was beginning to get worried. Seriously worried. It was becoming increasingly evident to her that the chick didn't just want to eat, it HAD to eat. It was growing weaker by the minute and its spirits were ebbing fast.

'Please hold on till your mum and dad get home. They really won't be long, I promise,' pleaded Nelly.

The Pipplewak chick sat lifelessly in its own gloop and stared vacantly through the bars of its cot. Nelly decided there was nothing for it. Favourite sweatshirt or no favourite sweatshirt, she would have to cheer the chick up with a cuddle. She reached over the bars of the cot, slid her fingers into the mustardy gloop and positioned themselves under the chick's bottom. With a heave and a squelch, she lifted the two-ton butterball off the sandsheet and cradled it in her arms.

She could feel its heart beating only faintly against her chest. There were more worrying signs, too. The lights were definitely fading in all three of the chick's eyes and its toes were beginning to droop.

'My goodness, it's going to die!' Nelly gasped. 'Please don't die on me!' she begged.

Nelly had never found herself in a situation like this before. What should she do? What could she do?

Every television hospital drama that she had

ever watched meteored through her mind. She didn't fancy mouth-to-beak resuscitation one bit, and even the prospect of a heart massage left her quaking in her socks.

'Don't go to sleep! You must stay awake!' she said, as the stalks of the chick's eyes began to wilt like dead flowers in a vase.

Nelly distinctly remembered one episode of *Scalpel City* when a child had been trapped beneath a building skip. The paramedics had had to wait for another skip delivery before they could free the boy and the trouble was, he was losing consciousness fast.

'*Stay awake, you must stay awake,*' one paramedic had said.

'*Or you may never regain consciousness,*' the other had whispered.

Nelly's arms were beginning to ache badly, but she gave the chick a little shake of encouragement and hoisted it closer to her chin.

'*Sing a song of sixpence, a pocket full of rye, four and twenty blackbirds baked* . . . maybe not,' said Nelly, chastising herself for the inappropriateness of her nursery rhyme.

The chick's eye-stalks responded positively to the gesture but then flopped back down on to its beak. It was fading fast.

Nelly turned to every corner of the room for help, but there was none on offer.

'I know,' she said loudly, fixing her sights on the shelf. 'Let's read your alphabet book together!'

The Pipplewak chick's eye-stalks raised slightly and then flopped limply back on to its beak.

'Stay awake, little fella, you must stay awake,' said Nelly, hurrying as fast as she could over to the far wall.

Roused slightly by the jogging motion, the chick lifted its head weakly and turned towards the shelf. Nelly could see the alphabet book, but she couldn't reach it, because both her arms were cradled under a gloop-encrusted bottom.

'I'm going to have to put you down for just a

moment,' she said softly. 'You can sit on my lap in just a tick.'

The chick offered no resistance as Nelly lowered it to the floor. Its legs folded like a broken deck chair and its beak dropped helplessly on to its chest. Nelly gulped bravely and reached the nursery book down from the shelf.

There was no time to lose. In two shakes of a gog's tail she was sitting cross-legged on the floor with the Pipplewak chick cradled between her knees. She decided to dispense with the 'are you sitting comfortably' bit and cut straight to the first page.

'**A** is for **A**ppetite,' said Nelly, reading the first caption of the alphabet book and holding the first picture up for the chick to see. It was a picture of a cooker.

'We know what appetite is, don't we!' she smiled, turning to the next page of the book.

'**B** is for **B**reakfast,' read Nelly, holding up another picture of a cooker.

The sapphire-blue colour in the Pipplewak

chick's eyes began to return and its beak began to open. Nelly frowned thoughtfully to herself and turned a page again.

'**C** is for **C**runchy,' she read, raising the pages of the book to reveal a picture of a fridge.

The wings of the Pipplewak chick began to flutter and its heart began to race.

Nelly arched her eyebrows and flipped quickly through the next few pages.

D was for **D**inner (a picture of a cooker), **E** was for **E**xtremely hungry (a picture of a cooker and a fridge), **F** was for **F**ood (a range of cookers) and **G** was for **G**ourmet (a picture of an expensive fridge).

By page seventeen the Pipplewak chick's entire body was a tremble of excitement.

Nelly slapped her forehead with her hand. 'And **H** is for **H**ow could I be so stupid!' she cried.

Heaving the chick back into her arms, Nelly rose unsteadily to her feet and staggered into the kitchen.

'Grub's up,' she cheered, placing the chick on the floor in front of the cooker and standing back.

The chick rose unsteadily to its feet and clamped its beak tight on to the side of the cooker. Its eyes blazed cobalt blue and its toenails hooked like anchors into the floor.

Nelly stepped further back and shielded her eyes as the cooker frame suddenly buckled, the twisted metal groaned and the smoked glass panel of the cooker door shattered like a windscreen around her knees. Before the last shard of glass had even stopped bouncing, the Pipplewak chick was hoovering it up with its beak. With an ear splitting 'PPPPPPPPPEEEEEEEEEEEEEEEEEE-EEEEPPPPPPPPPPPPPPP!' it lunged at the cooker like a hungry velociraptor and tore off another mouthful of twisted metal with its beak.

Nelly watched the cooker control switches slide down its gizzard and then gasped as it devoured the hotplates in one crunch.

'It's saving its mum's Post-it note till last,' murmured Nelly, 'just like I do with my peas!'

With the cooker devoured, right down to the Post-it, the Pipplewak chick turned and homed in on the fridge.

Nelly covered her ears as the white enamel doors splintered in its jaws and the freezer compartment buckled within its beak. Plastic shrapnel flew as the salad tray splintered and glass shelves cracked as they folded with every chew.

'Yup, it definitely likes to leave the Post-its till last,' smiled Nelly.

The Pipplewak chick raised its beak to the ceiling and sent the final helping of fridge motor down its gizzard. With a flap of its four scrawny wings and shake of its feathery root bobbles, it sat contentedly down on the kitchen floor before popping the second Post-it note into its beak.

Nelly cradled the chick back in her arms and gently stroked its head. 'I thought I was going to lose you,' she whispered emotionally.

'BUUUUUUUUUUUUUUUUUUUUUUUUUUUUUUU-UUUUUUUUURPPPP!' responded the chick.

8

'IT'S A BOY!' trilled Bill.

'Is it?' said Nelly.

'HE'S AN EARLY BIRD INDEED!' trilled Millet. 'We're so sorry we weren't here when he hatched, Nelly, we really weren't expecting him till next Thursday.'

'A Pipplewak hatching early? It's unheard of!' trilled Bill. Nelly decided to keep the circumstances to herself.

Millet and Bill had returned home just minutes after the second Post-it had been devoured. Nelly had had no time to tidy the house and had only just summoned the courage to remove the gloopy doormat from the cot.

Millet and Bill weren't worried at all. They were beside themselves with joy.

'I'm sorry about your telephone,' said Nelly, heaving the chick into the proud wings of its father. 'I had a little accident with it.'

Millet picked up the broken pieces of phone and dropped them into her son's wide-open beak. 'We're going to vary Grozzle's diet as much as we can, Nelly; we think that's very important for a growing child, don't you? Have you seen all the different food we have in our cupboard?'

'You mean your garage?' said Nelly, remembering all the scrap metal and junk that was piled up behind the door in the kitchen.

'It's not a garage, Nelly, it's our food cupboard. You don't need garages if you can fly!' trilled Bill.

Nelly smiled. Everything was beginning to make sense. Grozzle hadn't tried to bite her arm off earlier, he had tried to eat her mobile phone. The back garden was a landing strip – 'And this?' asked Nelly, pointing to the mobile suspended above the cot.

'It's a baby-gro,' trilled Millet. 'We hang the

copper pipe snacks just out of reach so that it encourages the baby to grow taller.'

Millet pulled a piece of plumbing from the mobile and popped it fondly into Grozzle's open beak.

'If he keeps on eating like that, he'll be bigger than his dad in no time!' laughed Nelly, turning for the door. It was time for her to return home.

The proud Pipplewak parents followed Nelly to the front step. 'Thank you so much for taking such good care of Grozzle until we got home. If there's anything we can ever do for you in return, please don't hesitate to ask.'

Nelly waved their kind offer away with a smile but then wavered for a moment on the front step. She stared down at her feet for a moment and then dropped to her knees to pick up the torn pieces of Asti's note.

'Actually,' said Nelly, 'there is something you might be able to do for me. And my sister, too.'

'Name it!' trilled Bill.

'All right then!' laughed Nelly. 'I will!'

9

It was midnight that same day in Sweet Street.

Inside the darkness of Nelly's house, a whispered duel was in progress.

'Am,' whispered Nelly, in a voice just loud enough to carry down the hall.

'Aren't,' volleyed the second voice, returning fire from her own bedroom.

'Am.'

'Aren't.'

'Am.'

'Aren't.'

'Go to sleep!' roared Mum with a grizzly-bear growl. She was still fuming from the sight of Nelly's sweatshirt after she had returned home from the Pipplewaks' that afternoon.

'Good nightam,' shouted Nelly.

'Good nightaren't,' shouted Asti.

Outside, in the moonlit darkness of the garden, a conversation of a very different nature was in progress.

Barney, the black and white tom from next door was sitting shakily on the fence, holding court with a Siamese cat and a tabby.

'I'm telling ya, man, from this very day I am turning vegetarian. I mean, it was enough to shake me whiskers from their roots. There I was about six-thirty this evening, doin' ma fing, you know – shakin' me tail, struttin' me stuff – when I hear this faint peepin' sound coming from the conifer not ten strides from this fence. Mmmm, me finks. Playtime, me finks. A poor little defenceless sparrer, me finks, or maybe a little frush chick, fresh out of its shell and burstin' to make my acquaintance. Anyway, so I do what we cats do. I mosey on over to the conifer and make my ascent up the trunk. You know, nice and cool like. You know my style. So, there I am ten

branches up, following the peeps and tryin' me best to arrive unannounced when suddenly the peeps start getting louder. And louder and LOUDER. This ain't no sparrer, I'm finkin to meself, and it ain't no frush.

'What was it?' asked the Siamese.

'It was freakin' huge, that's what it was!' squeaked Barney. 'It was freakin' monstrous! Four humungous purple wings, a beak the size of a cat flap, long white legs, orange claws and its eyes! I'm tellin' ya, man, those eyes were the scariest fings on three stalks I have ever seen. Next fing I know it's got me by the tail and it's dangling me upside down!'

'It never has!' gasped the tabby.

' "Touch another bird and you're dog meat," it says to me,' trembled Barney. ' "I know where you live," it says.'

'It never does!' gasped the tabby.

'So that's it, man, I'm finished wiv birds,' Barney trembled. 'From now on, it's grass and dandelions for me.'

'Touch another bird and you're dogmeat!'

'Me too,' said the Siamese.

'And me,' echoed the tabby.

Back inside the house, Nelly yawned and buried her face snugly into her pillow. A day that had started not so well had finished remarkably satisfactorily. Well, almost finished . . .

'Am,' she whispered with a smile.

THE ALLIGATORS
AT FLAT 25A

1

'Can you monster sit for us for two minutes on Wednesday evening please, Nelly?'

'Two minutes?' said Nelly. 'Don't you mean two hours?'

'No, two minutes,' snip-snapped a mystery voice. 'Two minutes the first time and then if all goes well, perhaps three minutes the second time and then if we're really making good progress we could work our way up from there.'

Of all the phone conversations Nelly had had with a mystery monster this had probably been her most intriguing to date. As always, the sound of a new monster had set her imagination racing, but it wasn't so much the snip-snapping sounds of the monster's voice that had got her thinking, it was more the conversation itself.

It was a damp and murky Monday evening in May. Nelly had just finished her tea and had been bracing herself for the threat of either rubber gloves or a tea towel, when the phone in her bedroom had mercifully rung. She had escaped full speed up the stairs, with Asti's protests ringing in her ears.

'Hello?' she had gasped, snatching up the phone and slamming it to her ear.

'Please don't say that,' the monster had replied. 'It's got the *L-word* in it. We would prefer it if you said "Hi" when you greet us.'

It was a weird request, but after nine months of monster sitting Nelly had become more than accustomed to weird.

'Hi,' she had duly responded.

'Hi,' the monster had snip-snapped. 'My name is Soar. It's good to speak to you, Nelly. I do so hope that you can help us.'

There had been a nervous pause before the

monster had continued and the conversation had become even stranger.

In between a series of snips and snaps Nelly had learned that Soar was an Altigator. He lived at altitude with his wife and newborn baby at Number 25A Éclair Towers, a high-rise block of flats that towered above the hospital on the north-eastern fringe of the Montelimar Estate. Nelly was always flattered to hear that news of her monster-sitting services was spreading and it was always nice to be wanted. But for *two minutes*? Surely there was some kind of mistake?

But Soar had been insistent. Two minutes was all that she was needed for. In fact it could be even less.

It was certainly a long way to go for such a short visit and most people probably would have declined. But Nelly wasn't most people. There was a quiver in the voice of the Altigator that told her that he genuinely needed her help. She had no idea why she was required for such a short visit, but one thing was certain – if she didn't make the journey to Éclair Towers, she was never going to find out!

'Of course I'll come over next Wednesday,' she smiled. 'What time would be good for you?'

'Six o'clock, Nelly; thank you so much. Six o'clock until two minutes past would be excellent for us!'

'Six o'clock it is then,' laughed Nelly. 'Is there anything special you would like me to bring?'

There was a pause, three snips and two snaps. 'High heels if possible,' said the Altigator. 'If you could possibly wear high heels it would be very much appreciated.'

It was Nelly's turn to pause now. High heels? This conversation was getting weirder and weirder.

'I'm afraid I haven't got any high heels, Soar,' explained Nelly. 'I've only got my school shoes or my trainers. I suppose I could borrow some high heels from my mum, but they're going to be a bit big for me.'

There was a pause, four snaps and two snips. 'Not to worry, Nelly,' snipped Soar. 'In that case, perhaps you could stand on tiptoes.'

That did it! This was officially and indisputably the strangest conversation Nelly had ever had with a monster at any time! Ever!

'I'll see you at six,' murmured Nelly.

'We look forward to it, Nelly,' snapped the Altigator. 'Hi and goodbye!'

When Nelly walked back downstairs to the kitchen she did so in a bit of a daze.

'Dad,' she mumbled.

'Where to this time?' sighed her dad, correctly anticipating another taxi request and handing her the tea towel in revenge.

'Éclair Towers,' said Nelly, picking a glass tumbler up from the drainer. 'Wednesday at six o'clock. But this time I'm going to need you to wait for me.'

'How long for?' exclaimed her dad, who still hadn't got around to having a taxi meter fitted to the Maestro.

'Two minutes,' murmured Nelly, with a squeak of tea towel on tumbler. 'Two minutes or . . . er . . . maybe less.'

2

Art classes after school on Wednesday meant that Nelly had far less time than usual to get ready for her monster-sitting visit. She flew upstairs at five-thirty, leaving her blazer and schoolbag discarded across the floor.

She tinkered with the contents of her wardrobe for a moment, wondering whether it was worth the effort of putting on her sardine sweatshirt for such a short visit. But after a bit of umming and aahing she persuaded herself that she should start as she meant to go on. After all, Soar had hinted that there could be more visits to come, and anyway, monster sitting wasn't quite monster sitting without her favourite monster-sitting sweatshirt.

And so, on went the sweatshirt, out came the

green jeans, red trainers and purple scrunchee. Before her schoolbag had barely had time to slide across the hall carpet and topple over by the mirror, Nelly was back downstairs and ready to roll.

Her dad wasn't. He was picking his teeth with a matchstick.

'Come out,' he gurgled, trying to dislodge something from a crevice between two molars.

'I've told you before not to eat the bones in the bacon rashers,' said Mum. 'You're worse than a dog.'

'But they're tasty,' dribbled Nelly's dad, whose lust for all things meaty had got the better of him this time. 'And they're soft.'

'You're the one that's soft,' said Nelly's mum. 'Soft in the head. Five rashers you've had. Five rashers of Freshco's thick-cut meaty pork back bacon and still you have to eat the bones. I'm surprised you didn't ask me for the wrapper to lick.'

'Gotcha!' said Dad, withdrawing the matchstick

from his mouth and removing the tiny white bone fragment. With a pleased-as-punch smile, he carefully popped it into place between his front teeth and nibbled it into submission.

'Worse than a dog, you are!' repeated Mum.

'Woof!' laughed Nelly's dad.

Nelly hovered by the front door and whistled.

'Here boy!' she said, patting her knees with both hands. 'It's time to visit the Altigators.'

Nelly's dad looked at his watch, barked twice and then went to fetch his car keys.

'You can have your tea when you get back, Nelly,' smiled her mum. 'There's bacon if you want it, or some left-over moussaka.'

'Woof,' barked Nelly, who was less than a fan of reheated aubergine.

'Bacon it is, then,' said Mum.

Nelly's dad returned from the lounge with the car keys dangling from his mouth and pushed the joke all the way to the front door.

'Come on then, Nelly,' he said. 'Let's do this thing.'

'Won't be a min,' said Nelly, quickly scribbling the Altigators' address and phone number on a Post-it and slapping it fast to the mirror in the hall.

'Why *am* I doing this?' she sighed to herself. 'By the time I get there it will be time to come back!'

The answer was an obvious one.

'Because I'm Nelly the Monster Sitter, that's why!'

When Nelly emerged from the house, Dad was sitting in the car with the engine running. 'Éclair Towers,' said Nelly, climbing into her seat. 'And make it snappy!'

The joke was lost on Dad, but he had enough prime pork rashers inside him to move through the gears with gusto.

'Slow down!' said Nelly as he sped the length of Sweet Sweet and then hung a rally driver's left into Milkbottle Close.

'Sorry,' said Dad, easing his foot off the accelerator. 'Have you monster sat for the Altigators before, Nelly?'

Nelly shook her head. 'First time,' she said.

'So what are you dropping off?' asked her dad, turning right into Caramel Way.

'I'm not dropping anything off,' said Nelly. 'They only want me to monster sit for two minutes.'

Nelly's dad screeched the car to a halt and placed his forehead on the steering wheel. 'Say that again,' he said.

'They only want me to monster sit for two minutes,' said Nelly, a little sheepishly. 'But next time it could be as long as three minutes!'

Nelly's dad raised his head then tapped it lightly again and again against the wheel.

'Why do they only want you for two minutes?' he asked incredulously, as they rejoined the early-evening high street rush hour.

'I don't know,' said Nelly. 'But I aim to find out.'

Nelly gazed through the windscreen as the car crawled past the charity shop. She could see Éclair Towers looming on the horizon at the far end of the road. It stuck up above the skyline like an ugly Lego block, and was set back from the road about a quarter of a mile from the shops.

From a distance, Éclair Towers seemed to have very little going for it. It had been built in the 1960s and seemed to have been crumbling ever since. For the citizens of Lowbridge fortunate enough not to live there it had become one of those things that you just lived with and simply managed to blot from your consciousness. In that respect, not too dissimilar to Asti.

'I'm surprised they haven't pulled it down,' said Nelly's dad, craning his eyes up and over the hardware store. 'It's a blooming eyesore if you ask me.'

'You can't pull it down, people live there!' exclaimed Nelly.

'Not from choice they don't,' said her dad.

Nelly fell silent for a moment and fixed her eyes on the levels of the tower that were visible above the roofline of the high street. Washing hung like dish cloths from small balconies and the walls of the tower were carbuncled with satellite dishes. The windows were square and lifeless and the masonry dingy and grey. Even from a distance there was something a bit desperate about Éclair Towers.

After a creeping, crawling, stop start journey up the high street, Nelly and her dad finally reached the Pontefract Roundabout.

'Won't be long now,' said Nelly's dad, looking at his watch. It was seven minutes to six.

Nelly smiled and flipped her passenger mirror down to make sure that she looked presentable. The car full-circled and then left the roundabout at the third exit. Éclair Towers loomed into view.

Close up, all of Nelly's worst suspicions were confirmed. The tower was an eyesore from top to bottom. Drab, grey and uncared for, it reared up into the sky with all the charm and personality of a breeze block.

'Aren't you glad you live in Sweet Street?' said her dad, steering the car towards a residents-only parking zone.

Even from a distance there was something a bit desperate about Eclair Towers.

Nelly nodded and then waved out of the window at a group of children who went to her school.

'I know them,' she said. 'And them!' she waved. 'They're really nice kids!'

'Nice kids, shame about the place,' said Dad, pulling the car up outside the entrance to the flats.

Nelly unclipped her seatbelt and sprung the handle on the door. 'I'll be five minutes,' she said. 'Six, if the flat is as high up as I think it is!'

'It's hardly worth turning the engine off,' sighed her dad.

Nelly skipped towards the entrance of the flats and stopped at the door. It had an entry phone panel with enough buttons to confuse a robot. Starting at the bottom she ran her eyes up in ascending order of flat numbers. Just as she expected, Flat 25A was located on the very top floor of the tower.

With a tingle of excitement, she pushed the button.

There was a pause, a crackle like a crisp packet and then a muffled snip-snap.

'Hi, who's there?' said a voice.

'Hel— I mean *Hi*, it's Nelly. Can I come up?'

'Hi, Nelly, glad you could make it!' snip-snapped the voice. 'Push the door, I'll meet you on the top floor.'

Nelly waited for the door to buzz and then heaved it open with her shoulder. She stepped into the entrance hall and turned as the door swung to like a bank-vault door and slowly closed with a click.

The entrance hall to the flats was a depressing to say the least. Graffiti scarred the walls and the stairwell whiffed of wee.

I'll take the lift, thought Nelly, spotting a buttoned panel on the far left of the hall. The brown metal doors of the lift were spaghettied with graffiti too, but at least as Nelly pressed the button, the lift mechanism sprung to life. It would have been a long walk up to the twenty-fifth floor!

Dad was right, she thought. This really is a miserable place to live.

With a clunk and a shudder, the lift doors opened. Nelly held her nose. More wee.

Dad was right, she thought. This really is a miserable place to live.

With another firm press of a button, the doors closed and the lift began its ascent to the top floor.

Nelly raised herself up on to tiptoe.

'Going up!' she smiled.

3

Nelly peered inquisitively at the graffitied panels that surrounded her. Apparently *Loz woz ere, Ryan was ere, Trudy* loved *John, Jaz* was a *bleep, Ben* was a *bleep bleep, Man U* were *bleep,* and *Nutta* couldn't spell.

Nelly glanced at her watch and then stared at the illuminated panel above the doors. The twenty-first floor was approaching. Twenty-one, twenty-two, twenty-three, twenty-four . . . *kerdunk* . . . twenty-five.

With a clunk and a shudder, the lift rattled to a halt and the battered metal lift doors slid open.

Nelly held out her hand, but there was no one waiting to greet her. She poked her head out of the lift and looked left. The twenty-fifth floor wasn't at all what she was expecting. To her amazement it was graffiti free. Wooden parquet tiles sparkled with floor polish and a sheen of fresh magnolia paint added a light and airy lustre to the walls.

Located about fifteen paces away to her right was the door to Flat 25A. It was painted a cheerful sky-blue colour and had a glass spyhole the size of a saucer positioned at head height. The door to the flat was shut fast, but as Nelly stepped out of the lift, it began to open with a slow, cautious creak.

Nelly double took, triple gasped and quadruple gulped.

As the door swung open, the long green jaws of a towering reptile ducked beneath the door frame and lumbered into view. He was thickly set with powerful, white-scaled arms and an armour-plated chest of thick, leathery hide. In the centre of his head was a huge orange eye, and at the bottom of both legs was a pair of high, platform shoes.

'Top of the evening to you, Nelly!' roared the

'Top of the evening to you, Nelly'

long, green, slender jaws. 'I'm Soar, this is my partner, Rise, and this is our new arrival, Summit.'

At least, that's what Nelly thought he said. It was difficult to tell because as the door of the flat opened the landing shook with the blare of rock music.

'Hi!' shouted Nelly, tiptoeing across the landing to greet her first Altigators.

Soar stepped to one side and courteously made room for his wife to squeeze through. She was a sight to behold too. The scales on her head glittered emerald green, her powerful, scaled legs were bowed like an alligator's and her high-heeled shoes gleamed a patent cherry-red. Cradled in her arms and screaming with all the decibels of a banshee was their baby Altigator son, Summit.

Nelly's senses reeled. Having been reassured by the magnolia paint, she now found herself rattled to her socks. With gritty determination she tiptoed boldly to the door.

On arrival at the entrance to the flat she was

surprised and a little shocked to be immediately handed baby Summit.

'There you go, Nelly,' snapped Rise, pressing the wriggling bundle into her chest and stepping on to the landing with Soar. 'We won't be a moment.'

Nelly didn't know what to say, and so with both arms full and her ears ringing, she watched instead.

Rise lumbered forward and joined Soar by the door. Soar turned his long, green snout towards her and gently squeezed her hand. No words were spoken, no snips were snapped. After a pause and a couple of deep, chest-buckling breaths, both Altigators turned towards the stairwell and strode across the floor. At the top of the stairwell they stopped, counted to three on their fingers and then simultaneously looked down.

That was it. With top to toe shudders they turned and lumbered quickly back to their flat.

'I'll take him now, Nelly,' snipped Rise. 'Could you come again the same time tomorrow?'

Nelly handed over the wriggly bundle and then

stepped to one side as the Altigators returned to their flat and closed the door.

Nelly stood for a moment in stunned disbelief. That really was it! She had just broken the world record for speed baby sitting! She turned to the Altigators' front door and peered at the spyhole, but it was impossible to see if she was being watched from the other side.

With an uneasy wave at the number 25 and letter A she turned and headed for the lift.

Her dad wasn't going to believe this. *She* couldn't believe this!

Nelly stood in confused silence as the lift descended to ground level. She was so taken aback by the Altigators' behaviour that she had completely forgotten that she was still standing on tiptoe.

'Have you hurt your feet?' asked her dad, as she tottered back to the car.

Nelly stared blankly into the car at him and then dropped back down on to her heels.

'How weird was that?' she mumbled.

* * *

As Nelly munched on her bacon rashers that evening she turned the Altigators' behaviour over and over in her mind.

'Perhaps they didn't like the look of you,' laughed Asti. 'Perhaps they thought, Aarrrrrrrrr-ggggghhhhh! It's a hideously ugly human! We can't subject our poor defenceless baby to that! I mean, *I* can't stand the sight of you for *one* minute, let alone *two*!'

'If they didn't like the look of me, then why did they ask me to go back tomorrow as well?' said Nelly, refusing to be goaded into a fight.

Asti didn't have an answer to that one.

There's something weird going on in that flat, thought Nelly. And I mean to find out what it is.

4

It was her mum who donned the taxi hat the following evening. Nelly's dad had refused to repeat the journey on the grounds that it was a complete waste of petrol and that too much rush-hour traffic in two days would be bad for his health.

Nelly's mum had countered that compared with bacon bones, rush-hour traffic fumes was positively nutritious, and anyway, she could put the petrol to good use by stopping off at Freshco along the way to buy some more aubergines.

Although the prospect of aubergines was a worry, Nelly was pleased to be getting a lift. Squally showers had been dowsing the Estate all through the day and she really didn't fancy arriving at the Towers damp or squelchy.

With the aubergines deposited in a carrier bag by her feet and the windscreen wipers squeaking like demented guinea pigs, Nelly and her mum inched their way further up the high street.

'I must say, Nelly,' said her mum, 'I do think the Altigators have got a bit of a cheek asking you to monster sit for just two minutes.'

'It'll be three minutes this evening,' said Nelly, springing to their defence.

'Big deal,' said her mum, distracted momentarily by a dress in a boutique window reduced to next to nothing by a *Summer Madness Cut-price Loopy Loo Sale.*

Nelly stared up the high street at the drizzled outline of Éclair Towers.

'The thing you have to understand about monsters,' she said, pushing the aubergines to one side with her foot, 'is that sometimes monsters do things that we don't understand.'

Nelly's mum inched forward again and switched her sights to the shoe shop.

Nelly looked at her watch. It was quarter to six.

'Are they like alligators?' asked her mum, prompted to ask the obvious question by the sight of a pair of fake crocodile shoes *slashed to £19.99*. 'I mean, Altigator does sound a bit like alligator, doesn't it?'

Nelly nodded. 'They are a bit like alligators,' she said, 'except they haven't got tails, they've only got one eye and they walk on two legs.'

Nelly decided not to mention the platform shoes.

'How old is their baby?' asked Mum, surging a whole car's length up the high street in one go and then grinding to a halt.

'I didn't get time to ask,' said Nelly, 'but he didn't look very old at all.'

Nelly's mum put her foot down again and eased the car further ahead.

'Once we clear the roundabout we'll be fine,' she said, with a glance at her wristwatch.

It was a further five minutes before they reached the top of the high street and if they hadn't cleared the roundabout so easily, Nelly would have been tempted to leap from the car and run the final quarter of a mile to the Towers.

'Thanks, Mum!' she smiled, stepping out of the Maestro into the parking zone. 'I'll be back in about seven minutes.'

Nelly's mum waved and then sat back in her seat to survey the rather dismal surroundings.

'I'm glad we don't live here,' she shuddered.

The school friends that Nelly had waved to the day before were nowhere to be seen this evening. Perhaps they had been driven indoors by the showers. A group of older children who Nelly didn't know had braved the rain and were sitting on a high wall close to the main entrance.

As Nelly walked past them they raised cigarettes to their mouths and eyed her with suspicious scowls. Nelly kept her eyes fixed to the ground and walked purposefully to the main entrance.

As she pushed the button to Flat 25A, the gang of kids behind her erupted into an aggressively loud prattle of laughter and swear words.

I'm glad I don't live here, thought Nelly.

The moment she pushed the button to enter the Towers, a face pressed itself flat to the tiny square window in the door and grinned broadly back at her through the glass. Nelly drew her head back sharply to refocus and then smiled. It was the red hair and freckled face of Connor Laing, one of her friends from school. Connor pressed the entry button from his side of the door and then stepped away from the window to make way for the auburn fringe of Hayley Burrows.

Nelly heaved the door open with her shoulder and then darted back to confirm her arrival to Soar. 'My friends have let me in, Soar. I'm on my way up!' she hollered.

Soar's voice snip-snapped and crackled a welcome through the intercom, informing Nelly that he would meet her on the top floor as before.

'What are you doing here?' said Hayley, as Nelly lurched back into the entrance hall and closed the door to with a shove of her bum.

'I'm visiting some friends upstairs,' Nelly explained.

'What are you doing here?'

'I like your sweatshirt,' said Connor. 'It's cool.'

'Thanks,' said Nelly, mindful that she wouldn't have long to chat, but anxious not to appear rude.

Hayley and Connor were standing amongst a group of other children, some of whom Nelly recognised, others that she didn't. Most of them were about her age, but a handful were considerably younger.

'Did they say anything to you?' said Hayley, peering anxiously out of the small, square pane of the window at the gang of kids outside.

Nelly threw a glance back in the direction she had come and shook her head.

'No, why?' she asked.

'Cos they're trouble,' said Connor. 'They think they rule this estate.'

'They *do* rule this estate,' said Hayley.

Nelly looked at her watch. It was bang on six o'clock and the Altigators would be waiting.

'Don't the flats have a caretaker?' she asked. 'You know, someone to keep an eye on things?'

Hayley shook her head. 'There used to be one

living there,' she said, nodding towards the door of Flat 1B, 'but they only last about a week and then they get too frightened to stay.'

Nelly placed her hand on Hayley's arm and then stepped towards the lift.

'Look, Hayley, I've just got to go and see my friends and then I'll be right down. Give me five minutes and you can tell me all about those kids outside, yeah?'

'You'll need longer than five minutes,' grumbled Connor, peering through the window and then suddenly ducking down.

'I'll be as quick as I can,' said Nelly, stepping into the lift.

As the lift doors closed a weight of responsibility began to bear down on her shoulders. At the top of Éclair Towers it seemed a family of Altigators were strangely in need of her assistance and now at the bottom of the Towers her friends and their friends seemed strangely out of sorts too. Éclair Towers appeared to be a troubled place from top to bottom.

She turned to the graffiti-soaked walls of the lift. *Razor woz ere, Chaz woz ere, Nutta* was now *king, Gaz woz a bleep bleep, Sharon rocks* and *Ben* was a *bleep bleep bleep.* Nelly shook her head. If the lift was a movie, the censors would have had to give it an eighteen certificate.

She was pleased to step out at the twenty-fifth floor, and even more pleased to be greeted face to face by the Altigators. This time they had ventured out on to the landing to meet her, leaving the door of their flat ajar. Loud rock music was blaring through the gap between the door and the door frame forcing Soar to open his jaws wide to speak above it.

'Top of the evening to you again, Nelly,' roared Soar. 'We really do appreciate you coming.'

'It's such a long way to come for such a short visit,' agreed Rise, snapping her emerald green jaws shut like a bulldog clip.

Nelly smiled, a little reassured by the fact that the Altigators at least seemed to be aware of their own eccentricity.

'Now then,' snapped Soar. 'Shall we proceed with stage two?'

Rise nodded nervously, patted Summit tenderly on the head and handed the screaming bundle to Nelly. Nelly looked down into the gaping gums of the baby Altigator. His teeth had yet to come through but his epiglottis was buzzing like a kazoo.

'Would you carry Summit over to the door please, Nelly, and perhaps turn your back,' snip-snapped Rise. 'We wouldn't want our antics to frighten him, would we?'

Nelly blinked blankly at the wriggling bundle of claws, jaws and blankets.

With a slightly bewildered nod, she took the bundle in her arms and tiptoed towards the door of Flat 25A.

'Let's go,' said the determined but strangely nervous voice of Soar behind her.

'Ready when you are,' faltered Rise.

Nelly stood motionless, facing the door of the flat. OK, it was very clear that the Altigators didn't want their baby to see what they were about to do, but did that mean that Nelly wasn't entitled to watch, either?

She did the decent thing and stared at the brass numbers on the door. She studied the screws that had fixed them to the wooden panelling and then traced the contours of each numeral and letter with her eyes. But it was no good. She just *had to* turn round and see what the Altigators were doing!

Careful to keep baby Summit's eyes shielded from view, Nelly craned her head around slowly.

Soar and Rise were standing at the top of the stairs, holding hands. After a count of three, they looked down and then wavered. After a count of four, they looked down and then faltered. And then after a count of ten, they looked down and then gave up.

'It's hopeless,' snapped Soar, breaking loose from Rise's hand and clomping back in his green platform shoes towards the door of the flat.

'It's pointless,' snipped Rise, turning with a

'It's hopeless.'

stomp of her cherry-red high heels and trudging miserably after him.

Nelly stood with baby Summit wriggling in her arms and then lifted him back into the powerful embrace of his mother.

'I'm so sorry, Nelly,' snapped Soar. 'This is hopeless and pointless. We shan't be requiring your services again. Goodbye.'

Nelly scratched her head.

'But what about stage three?' she asked, not even sure what stages one and two were.

Rise opened the door of the flat and stepped inside, with Summit cradled in one arm.

'There won't be a stage three now, Nelly,' she shouted, above the thumping racket of the rock music. 'Thank you so much for visiting us again, hi and goodbye.'

Before Nelly could enquire further, the door to Flat 25A closed in her face. Her monster-sitting visit was over.

Nelly turned towards the lift and slipped her hands into her pockets. If she was confused the evening before, she was doubly puzzled now.

She slapped her finger against the button to call the lift and turned back towards the door of 25A with a shrug. She felt like she had failed, like she had somehow let the Altigators down. She didn't know how or why, but as the lift doors opened, she had never felt so determined about anything.

'I'll be back,' she murmured.

5

When she stepped out of the lift at ground-floor level, Connor, Hayley and their group of friends were still gathered around the stairwell.

'Is it still raining?' said Nelly, assuming that the weather was keeping them indoors.

'No, but there are still six big drips sitting on that wall,' said Connor, pressing his face to the glass pane in the front door.

'We're not going outside while they're there,' said Hayley. The rest of her friends nodded their agreement.

Nelly frowned and strode across the entrance hall to join Connor.

'The one in the middle, smoking the cigar, is Nutta,' said Connor. 'He's bad news if you cross him and bad news if you don't.'

Nelly squeezed her cheek alongside Connor's and peered through the window. Her mum was waiting for her in the car park and would be expecting her to emerge from the flats at any minute.

'He looks a bit of a nutter,' said Nelly, switching her attention to the wall. 'What does he think he's doing, smoking cigars? He only looks about fifteen!'

'He thinks it makes him look big,' said Connor.

'He is big!' said Hayley, joining them at the door.

Hayley had a point. The cigar-puffing Nutta holding court in the middle of the wall was only fourteen years old. But what he lacked in years and brains, he more than made up for in muscles and forehead.

'That's the other gang leader,' said Connor, periscoping his finger over the sill of the window and pointing across the car park. 'His name's Syko. And believe me, he IS!'

Nelly turned her head away from the wall and

watched as a tall, shaven-headed boy began weaving a swaggering path through the car park, idly twanging every car aerial within reach.

'He better not do that to our car or my mum will kill him,' Nelly murmured.

Luckily for Syko, his route through the car park took him away from the Morton family Maestro and past the burnt-out wreckage of a Ford Orion instead.

'His whole family are psychos,' said Hayley. 'I'm glad they don't live on our floor.'

As Nelly peered through the small glass pane of the entrance door she was suddenly overcome by a mixture of guilt and relief. Her relief at being able to climb into the car with her mum and drive away from Éclair Towers was hugely undermined by her guilt at leaving her friends behind. She suddenly felt incredibly lucky and privileged to live where she lived, because there were no Nuttas or Sykos hanging like gorillas from the trees of Sweet Street and no spray cans *wozzing* and *bleeping* across the walls.

'I must be going,' she whispered, apologetically. 'My mum is waiting for me outside.'

'See you tomorrow in school, Nelly, yeah?' said Hayley cheerfully.

'Sure,' said Nelly, heaving the door open with both arms.

'And if they say anything to you, just ignore them,' cautioned Connor.

'I will,' said Nelly.

Nelly stepped outside to the smell of damp concrete. The rain had long stopped but a musty wetness seemed to have seeped deep into the concrete of the Towers. There was the whiff of fish and chips too, courtesy of a screwed-up, vinegar-drenched wrapper discarded thoughtlessly at the base of the entrance door.

Nelly glanced at the gang of boys skulking around the wall and then gave it large with a wave to her mum. The eyes of the gang flicked across the car park to the Maestro, clocked the adult inside and then slunk back to the wall.

Nelly ran to the car and prised open the door.

'How were the Altigators?' asked her mum, with a twist of the ignition key.

'Don't ask,' sighed Nelly.

'Explain,' said her mum, pointing the car back in the direction of the Pontefract Roundabout.

'That's precisely the problem,' sighed Nelly. 'I can't explain!'

6

That night, after a lengthy chinwag with her mum, Nelly hit upon a plan. She wouldn't wait for the Altigators to call again, she would call the Altigators herself. Right now, in fact.

She sat down on her bed and tugged the cord of her monster-sitting phone across the carpet. With eight taps of her finger she dialled the Altigators' number and leant back against her bedroom wall.

The dial tone registered but after eight rings there was no response at all. Nelly's hand loosened its grip on the receiver and prepared to abort the call, but just as she lowered the phone from her ear, there was a click.

She sprung the phone back to her ear and listened hard for a snip or a snap. There were three snips, four snaps and a very loud, 'HI, WHOIZZIT SPEAK UP AND UP AND UP!'

Soar was on the phone at the other end, trying to be heard above the noise of the rock music.

'HI, SOAR, IT'S NELLY,' shouted Nelly, thankful that she had closed her bedroom door. 'DO YOU THINK YOU COULD TURN THE MUSIC DOWN?'

'PARDON?' hollered Soar.

'CAN YOU TURN THE MUSIC DOWN!' hollered Nelly.

'NO,' snapped Soar.

It wasn't the answer Nelly was hoping for.

'I CAN'T HEAR YOU VERY WELL, SOAR,' hollered Nelly.

'SPEAK UP, NELLY, I CAN'T HEAR YOU VERY WELL,' shouted Soar.

There was a pause, a squeak of a door and then a welcome drop in rock volume.

'That's better,' snapped Soar. 'Sorry I took so long to answer the phone, Nelly, I couldn't hear it ringing above the sound of the music.'

Nelly sighed. 'That's OK, Soar,' she smiled, 'at least we can hear each other now.'

'That's because I'm standing by the lift,' said Soar. 'It's much quieter out here in the hallway.'

Nelly scratched her head. These Altigators were turning out to be nuttier than the nuttiest of Nuttas.

'Now then, Nelly, what can I do for you?' snapped Soar.

Nelly slid off her bed and began to pace around her room with the phone cord trailing after her.

'Soar, it's *me* that would like to do something for *you*!' she smiled. 'I want to come and monster sit for you again, but for longer than *three minutes*!'

Soar began to pace across the parquet floor with the phone cord trailing after him.

'Nelly, thanks for the offer, but that really won't be necessary. Rise and I have already tried our best.'

Nelly wound the phone cord around her finger and continued to pace.

'Tried what, Soar?' she asked. 'What exactly have you been trying your best to do?'

Soar wrapped the phone cord around his claw and continued to pace.

'To conquer our fear, Nelly,' he snipped.

Nelly faltered. That wasn't an answer she had been expecting.

'Your fear of what, Soar?' she asked gently.

There were no snips, no snaps; only an awkward, empty silence. It was as though even the mention of the problem was too much for the Altigator to bear. Nelly waited like a psychiatric counsellor for Soar to open his heart.

'Our fear of depths,' said Soar. 'We're Altigators. And all Altigators are afraid of depths. That's why we live at altitude.'

Nelly flopped like a dead weight on to her bed. Afraid of depths? What on earth did that mean? How could great hulking monsters like Altigators be afraid of anything?

'You're sure you don't mean heights?' asked Nelly. 'I've heard of people being afraid of heights.'

'HEIGHTS!' roared Soar. 'Goodness, no. We love heights, we adore heights! That's why we live in the top flat! No, believe me, Nelly, altitude is tops for Altigators!'

Nelly looked down at the tip of her index finger. She had twiddled the phone cord around it so many times that she had shut off the blood supply to her fingertip. As she began to unwind the cord, she slowly rewound the Altigators' peculiar behaviour through her mind.

Let's see . . . they live in a *top* flat, they don't say hel*lo* they say *hi*; they wanted me to wear *high* heels, or if not, *tip*toe, they say *top* of the evening to me, and always *hi* and goodbye. That's a lot of *tips, tops* and *highs.*

It was all beginning to make sense. *Kind of.*

'But what does being afraid of depths mean, Soar?' she said. 'If you don't mind me asking.'

Soar loosened the cord from his claw and continued.

'It means we can't look down and we can't use the stairs or the lift.'

Nelly gasped. 'What, never?'

'Never,' snapped Soar.

'But surely you can use the stairs and the lift to go *up*?' gasped Nelly.

'We live on the top floor, Nelly. The stairs and the lift don't go up any further.'

Nelly leapt from her bed and began to pace across the room again.

'So when I came to see you the first time . . .' she said.

'That was stage one,' explained Soar. 'Stage one was plucking up the courage to look down the stairs.'

'But you did it!' cried Nelly. 'Both of you managed to do it!'

'I know,' said Soar. 'We'd been practising in the lounge for weeks. But then it came to stage two.'

'Which was?' asked Nelly.

'Stage two was putting one foot *D-word* on to the first step.'

D-word? thought Nelly. He must mean putting one foot *down* on to the first step.

'Altigators don't say the *D-word*,' explained Soar.

Nelly replayed her last visit through her mind. She pictured the Altigators standing at the top of the stairs; the wavering, the faltering, the slumping of those powerful shoulders and the final desperation.

'We just couldn't do it,' sighed Soar. 'As hard as we tried, we just couldn't *L-word* our feet *D-word* on to that step.'

'*Lower* your feet *down* on to that step,' deciphered Nelly.

'And so you see, Rise and I won't be needing your services any more. Because we won't be going *D, L, B,* or *U* at any time in the future.'

Down, lower, beneath or *under,* figured Nelly.

'But how do you eat? How do you shop?' asked Nelly.

'Freshco Direct,' snapped Soar. 'They bring everything we need right up to us. Everything fresh though, nothing *D-word* frozen.'

'*Deep* frozen.' translated Nelly, placing her hand on her hip. She was fresh out of questions but she had mustered a trolley full of resolve.

'Soar,' she begged, 'you've got to let me help you. *Please* let me visit you again tomorrow. I'm sure I can help you conquer your fear of the *D-word*, and all the others. I've barely had a chance to get to know Summit, he looks so cute and adorable I'm sure we could have some wonderful times together. And I'd love to get to know Rise better too. *Pleaaaase,* Soar, let me come again tomorrow.'

Soar wavered in the hallway for a moment, wrapping the phone cord tightly around his claw and then further up and around the bulging, scaly bicep of his left arm.

'If you're an Altigator, Soar, then surely you shouldn't give *up*!' said Nelly, not entirely sure whether the logic of that gambit was entirely right.

'Or at least, if you're an Altigator, you musn't let a problem like this get you *down*,' she said, trying to cover herself in both directions.

Soar peered at the tattoo of an air balloon, emblazoned across his shoulder. It was totally enmeshed in phone cord.

'You're right, Nelly,' he finally snapped. 'You've persuaded me. We'll see you the same time tomorrow!'

'For longer than three minutes!' laughed Nelly.

'For as long as you wish to visit!' smiled Soar.

7

'Give me an hour!' said Nelly the following evening, as she climbed excitedly out of the Maestro and pointed herself in the direction of the Towers.

With a wink and a wave, her dad reversed the car away from the car park and then left her alone with her friends.

'That's where Syko's family live, in that flat there,' said Hayley, picking up on a conversation that she and Nelly had been having earlier that day at school. Nelly followed the direction of Hayley's pointing finger towards a line of dish cloths somewhere between the eighth and eleventh floors.

'And Nutta's family live right up there,' said Connor, skying his finger further up towards the roof.

'They've all been in prison,' said Hayley, 'even the grandmas.'

Nelly shook her head. 'Do they make things bad for you?' she asked.

'Not just us, everyone,' said Hayley. 'They spit and they swear and they cause fights . . .'

'And they pick on people and graffiti everything and break things.'

'And burn things,' said a smaller boy who had sidled alongside them to listen. Nelly followed his gaze to the burnt-out Orion car.

'If it wasn't for them, Éclair Towers could be a really nice place to live,' said Connor.

'It's not so bad,' said Hayley philosophically. 'There's loads of stairs to play on!'

The mention of stairs drew Nelly's thoughts back to the Altigators.

'I'll catch you later, OK?' she said. 'I've just got to visit my friends.'

'Sure!' said Hayley. 'We'll probably still be here, unless *you know who* come along.'

Nelly scanned the car park. There was no sign

of a Nutta or a Syko. 'See you in an hour!' she waved.

She ran to the main entrance of the Towers and pushed the button of Flat 25A. Soar's voice crackled through the intercom almost immediately, and enthusiastically beckoned her upstairs.

'I'm on my way!' she laughed, heaving the door open with her shoulder and stepping inside the entrance hall.

She was greeted by the familiar riot of graffiti-scrawled walls and that equally grim whiff of wee.

'Up, up and away,' she murmured as she punched the top-floor lift button with her finger.

She stood for a moment and then stabbed the button again. There was no familiar click and judder of a lift mechanism starting up and no light in the panel above the doors. She gave the button a double stab and then stood back.

The lift wasn't working.

She was going to have to walk up twenty-five floors!

With a groan and a mutter she turned and trudged towards the stairs. The whiff of wee grew stronger as she climbed the first step but thankfully faded away as she reached the next flight.

'One,' she counted under her breath. 'Only twenty-four to go!'

Step by step, flight by flight, she continued her journey up the stairwell. With the exuberance of youth on her side and the promise of a date with the Altigators at the end of the climb, she was making surprisingly easy work of it . . .

. . . until she reached floor seven. Nelly was just turning the corner of the stairwell and about to progress to floor eight when she heard the sound of echoed footsteps approaching from above. Not just footsteps, either: shouting, spitting, swearing and if she wasn't mistaken, the rattle of a spray can.

She braced herself for an unsavoury introduction.

Syko's bovver boot was the first to turn the corner of the stairwell. Scuffed, dirty and practically leather-free it looked completely kicked through to the steel toe-cap. It crunched down on to the step with the lumbering gait of a troll and then flattened with the arrival of the second boot.

Nelly stepped back. Her suspicions were about to be confirmed. Seven or eight other pairs of bovver boots were following close behind. What was she going to do? It was pointless going down. She decided to stand her ground.

As the rest of Syko's wiry frame loomed into view, a chorus of laughter and grunts followed him down. One by one, the rest of the gang lumbered around the corner, tumbling to a halt at the sight of Nelly.

'Choo lookinnat?' growled a mouth as wide as its accompanying forehead.

Nelly stared fearlessly up into Nutta's eyes.

'Nothing,' she said.

'Where are you going? You don't come from round here,' said Syko. 'What are you doing on our stairs?'

'Choo lookinnat?' growled a mouth as wide as its accompanying forehead.

'They're not your stairs,' said Nelly. 'They belong to the Towers.'

'Yeah, smart arse? Well, the Towers belong to US!' sneered Syko, pressing his nose stud millimetres from Nelly's face. 'Now if you want to keep breathing, answer the question. Where are you going?'

Nelly coughed deliberately, forcing Syko's nose stud to retreat.

'I'm visiting some friends of mine,' she said. 'They live on the top floor.'

A wave of surprise rippled through the gang.

'You mean the Weirdo floor?' said Nutta, with a guttural snort and a spit. 'I'm telling you, I ain't ever seen 'em but whoever lives up there is as weird as hell.'

Syko and the gang broke out into a cackle of grunts and laughter.

'Shall we decorate their walls for them again?' sniggered a pony-tailed thug with a rattle of a fluorescent-pink spray can.

Nutta shook his head. 'I'm not walking all the

way up there if the lift's broken,' he grunted. 'And anyway, the Weirdos keep painting over our art.'

Nelly smiled inwardly. The fresh magnolia paint made extra sense now.

'Hang on,' said Syko, pressing a knuckle either side of the wall and trapping Nelly somewhere in between. 'If you're going to see a Weirdo, then that must make you a Weirdo too!'

'YEAAAAAAAHHHHH!' chorused the gang. 'Are you a Weirdo too?'

'No,' said Nelly.

'Then why have you got *sardine* written on your sweatshirt?' logicked Nutta.

Nelly looked down at her chest. 'Because I like it,' she replied.

Syko folded at the elbows and drew his nose stud within polishing distance again.

'Well, I DON'T LIKE IT!' he growled. 'And do you know what? I DON'T THINK I LIKE YOU EITHER!' he glowered.

'Mutual, I'm sure,' said Nelly, ducking under

his arms and forging a path through the gang and up the stairs.

'Let her go,' growled Syko.

'Yeah, let the Weirdo go,' grunted Nutta.

Nelly strode purposefully on up to the eighth floor, her heart beating fast. She was twenty-one floors up and still counting before her pulse began to slow.

'Hayley and Connor are right,' she sighed. 'Nutta and Syko are bad news.'

8

There was better news waiting for her on floor twenty-five. Soar and Rise had decided to relax their tiptoe policy and were now happy for Nelly to walk on the flats of her feet.

'Much appreciated,' panted Nelly, whose fifty-flight journey up the twenty-five-floor stairwell had taken its toll on her calf muscles.

She dropped down on to the balls of her feet and followed Soar and Rise through the door of the flat.

'Summit's asleep in his cot,' snapped Rise, pushing the sky-blue door open with her claw.

Nelly's ears reverberated once again as rock music exploded from the room.

'Oh no he's not, he's woken up!' hollered Soar, lumbering over to the cot and scooping the baby Altigator up into his arms.

Small wonder, thought Nelly.

Her eyes darted to the cot and then skipped around the four corners of the flat. The Altigators seemed to be obsessed with height. The walls and ceiling were high. Two high-backed stools stood in the centre of the room next to a baby's high chair. A single shelf adorned with porcelain birds ran at high level right around the room. The flat was lit with hi-lighters. A high-level bunk bed was positioned in the far corner of the room and a rack of high, platform shoes stretched across the far wall. Somewhat surprisingly, though, there was no sign of the Altigators' hi-fi.

'MAKE YOURSELF HIGHLY AT HOME!' hollered Soar above the thumping bass of the rock music.

'THANKS!' screamed Nelly, hoisting herself up on to one of the stools.

'ACTUALLY,' she yelled, climbing back down off the stool, 'DO YOU THINK WE COULD GO BACK OUTSIDE INTO THE HALLWAY TO TALK? IT'S A BIT QUIETER OUT THERE!'

'GOOD IDEA!' hollered Rise.

And so no sooner had Nelly found herself inside the Altigators' flat, than she found herself outside again, standing beside the lift.

'The lift's not working,' she said, tapping the doors with her knuckle and then pointing to the lifeless panel above the doors.

'Never has done,' grumbled Soar. 'How can you call a lift a lift if it doesn't lift you?'

Nelly looked at the doors. 'When it *does* work it'll lift you if you're on one of the *L-word* floors.' (Lower floors.)

'Not much good to us,' grumbled Soar.

Nelly peered over a tangle of blankets at baby Summit. His eyes were closed and he was contentedly sucking his mum's index claw.

'He'll be asleep again soon,' said Rise, rhythmically bobbing up and down on her high heels like a ship at sea.

'Well, when he's asleep again,' whispered Nelly, 'let's see if we can crack stage two.'

The huge, powerful, green jaws of Soar turned

towards Rise and snapped to with a grimace. The two Altigators blinked at each other slowly and then looked back at Nelly with a shudder.

'Positive thoughts!' said Nelly, sensing that they weren't even going to try. 'You need to fill yourself with positive thoughts!'

Soar looked at Rise. Rise looked at Soar. Both of them looked positively negative.

'Think of me as your positive petrol pump,' said Nelly. 'All you need to do now is use me to fill up with five-star positivity!'

It was a strange thing to say, but it was the best she could think of at the time.

Rise looked at Nelly and then removed her index claw slowly from baby Summit's gums.

'I will if you will,' she snapped to Soar.

Soar took a deep breath and pumped out his chest. Baby Summit was sleeping, the stairwell was beckoning.

'All right then,' he said, with a clench of both knuckles, 'let's do it.'

Nelly punched the air, but resisted clapping

her hands in case baby Summit woke up.

'OK,' she said, sandwiching herself between the two Altigators and taking both of them by the hand. 'First of all, I want both of you to close your eye and think of something marvellous. Think of the most wonderful thing you can think of imaginable.'

The marble-veined hairy eyelids of the two Altigators slid shut and then opened again.

'Are we allowed to say what it is?' asked Soar.

'If you want,' nodded Nelly.

'An air balloon journey through space,' snipped Soar.

'An air balloon journey above Soar's air balloon journey,' snapped Rise.

'Fair enough,' smiled Nelly. 'Now close your eye again, keep thinking those positive thoughts, and on the count of five, I want you to walk with me to the stairwell. And don't worry, I won't let you walk too far.'

Soar and Rise closed their eyes and raised their jaws to the ceiling. Nelly began to count, but by the time she'd got to *two*, the Altigators' grip on

her fingers was so strong, she had to stop.

'You're crushing my fingers!' she squeaked.

'Sorry, Nelly,' said Rise, 'I'm a bit nervous.'

'Me too,' snapped Soar.

The Altigators relaxed their grip on Nelly's hands and Nelly picked up the count at three . . .

'Four . . . You're squeezing again!'

'Sorry.'

'Sorry.'

'. . . You're still squeezing . . . still squeezing . . . Five!'

The Altigators relaxed their grip as best they could and waited nervously for Nelly to instruct them further.

'OK,' said Nelly. 'Remember, keep those five-star positive thoughts flowing through your minds. We're going to walk to the stairwell now.'

Nelly stepped forward and then sprung back. Soar and Rise's arms had stiffened like lampposts and the soles of their platform shoes had welded themselves to the floor.

'Come on, you two!' said Nelly. 'This is the easy bit. You know you can do it, I've seen you do it before!'

Soar's single eye flickered open and then slammed shut at the sight of the stairwell.

'I'm thinking about stage two!' he snapped.

'Me too,' snipped Rise.

'Well, don't!' tutored Nelly. 'Think about air balloons and deep space. Oops! I mean, think about space. Forget about the deep bit.'

'Stop saying deep,' snapped Soar.

'Sorry,' said Nelly.

'Count to five again,' said Rise, unwelding the soles of her high heels.

'Only if you promise not to squeeze,' said Nelly.

'I promise,' said Rise.

'Me too,' snapped Soar.

Nelly counted to a squeeze-free five and together the three of them took one step forward.

'You see!' said Nelly. 'You *can* do it! Now this time, keep walking till I say stop.'

There was a moment of leaden reluctance, but after a tug from Nelly the two Altigators made stiff-legged progress to the top of the stairwell.

'Positively excellent!' said Nelly. 'Now, before you open your eyes I want you to look *D-word*.' (Down.)

The emerald and white scales of the Altigators shivered with revulsion, but bolstered by full tanks of five-star positivity, they slowly drew the tips of their jaws downwards.

'OK, open your eye,' said Nelly.

Each Altigator opened their eye in turn, but as they did so, Nelly closed hers and began buckling at the knees.

'You're squeezing, YOU'RE SQUEEZING!' she squeaked, contorting her body to try and wrestle her hands free from the Altigators' bone-crushing grip.'

'I CAN'T HELP IT! I CAN'T HELP IT!' snipped Rise.

'IT'S A STEP! IT'S A STEP!' snapped Soar.

'CLOSE YOUR EYES AGAIN! CLOSE YOUR EYES AGAIN!' gasped Nelly, tears running down her cheeks.

The Altigators' furry eyelids slammed shut, and their grips on Nelly's hands loosened.

Nelly gave her fingers a little wriggle to check that they hadn't broken, and then took two deep, exasperated breaths.

'Now then. Keep thinking those positive thoughts. We're not going to give up now after coming this far. Keep your eyes closed and get ready for stage two. AND NO SQUEEZING!' she said.

'Sorry, that was me,' said Rise.

'It was *both* of you,' said Nelly. 'OK, on the count of three we're all going to step forward and *L-word* our foot *D-word* on to the step *B-word*, but as you do, I want you to imagine you are stepping *D-word* into your wonderful hot-air balloons for the first time.'

'I stepped *up* into *my* hot-air balloon,' whispered Soar.

'So did I,' whispered Rise.

Nelly sighed. 'Look, come on, the two of you. You can do this, you really can. Summit won't be asleep for ever, this is our big chance.'

Rise determinedly clenched her claws into fists.

'Do it for Summit!' said Nelly.

'We will!' snapped Soar. 'We must!' he snipped.

Nelly gave both Altigators' hands a squeeze of encouragement, and then began her countdown.

'And remember, be positive, think positive. Don't think of it as stepping *D-word.* Think of it as stepping *F-word – forward.* Remember you are not *L-wording* your foot, you are *P-wording – placing* your foot. Not *D-word* on to the next step but *O- and V- T-word – on the very top* of the next step.'

'I'm stepping forward and placing my foot on very top of the next step down,' said Soar.

'Don't say *down*!' said Nelly. 'Say *there.* Now, let's say it together.'

'We're stepping *forward* and *placing* our feet *on the very top* of the next step *there*.'

'Again, louder!' said Nelly.

'WE'RE STEPPING *FORWARD* AND *PLACING* OUR FEET *ON THE VERY TOP* OF THE NEXT STEP *THERE*!'

'Even louder!' cried Nelly, rallying her troops like a cheerleader.

'WE'RE STEPPING *FORWARD* AND *PLACING* OUR FEET *ON THE VERY TOP* OF THE NEXT STEP *THERE*!' chanted the Altigators.

'OK, this time we do it for real!' whooped Nelly. 'After three: one . . . two . . . three!'

'WE'RE STEPPING FORWARD AND PLACING OUR FEET ON THE—**I'VE DONE IT**!' whooped Soar.

Nelly lurched half forward and half backwards as Soar stepped forward but Rise stayed resolutely put.

'I can't do it!' shuddered Rise, breaking free from Nelly's grasp and running back into the flat. 'It's too *deep* and *low* and *down*!'

Nelly stared back from the top of the step and watched as Rise came back out of the door, cradling Summit in her arms.

'You see, he's woken up now, I told you it would be too frightening for him.'

Nelly turned her head to her left. Soar was standing there, looking particularly pleased with himself.

'YOU SEE, NELLY! I STEPPED FORWARD AND PLACED MY FOOT ON THE VERY TOP OF THE NEXT STEP THERE!' he snapped.

'YOU SEE, SOAR!' said Nelly. 'I told you you

could do it. It's all about positive thinking. Now, are you ready to try the next step!'

The purple vein in the side of Soar's neck flexed and his powerful jaws snapped shut with a gulp.

'Er, no, Nelly,' he wavered, stepping the one step back up into the hallway. 'I think that's quite enough positive petrol for one day.'

Nelly smiled. It wasn't exactly a huge leap for monsterkind, but at least they had made one small step in the right direction.

'OK,' she said. 'We'll save stage three for tomorrow!'

'Same time?' said Soar, strutting like a rooster back to the door of the flat.

'It's Saturday tomorrow,' said Nelly. 'Why don't I come at lunchtime, say twelve?'

Soar nodded. 'Twelve will be fine.'

'I might be a few minutes late if the lift still isn't working!' laughed Nelly.

The blare of rock music blasted from the door as the Altigators returned to their flat. Nelly waved to them from the top of the stairwell and then turned to begin her descent to the ground floor.

'It's a lot easier walking down than up!' she laughed again as she skipped past the graffitied landing of floor twelve. 'I don't know what all the fuss is about!'

She injected some caution into her step at floor eight, but was relieved to find the staircase Syko- and Nutta-free. In fact, the entire staircase was empty from top to bottom and so too was the ground-floor entrance hall. Hayley and Connor were nowhere to be seen and even the wall outside the Towers was deserted too.

Nelly looked at her watch. She had twenty minutes to kill before her mum was due to return. Should she hang around the flats or start walking?

'Oi! Sardine!' shouted a distant voice from a distant row of bottle banks.

Syko and Co. had spotted her.

Nelly briskly started walking.

9

She was half way along Eclair Way when her mum drew up alongside her in the Maestro.

'How did you get on?' she asked, as Nelly climbed into the car.

'Good!' said Nelly. 'Very good, in fact!'

With the rush hour past and the roads clear, Nelly and her mum made rapid progress back to the house. Nelly had barely had time to mull over her stage-three strategy for the next day before she was confronted with an unforeseen dilemma at home.

Reheated aubergine.

Nelly sat alone at the dinner table and lifted the lid of the oven-proof dish. Considering everyone else had already eaten, there seemed an awful lot of moussaka left. There were two obvious reasons for this. The first was her mum's vegetarian insistence on a complete absence of minced lamb. The second was her mum's vegetarian insistence on compensating for an absence of minced lamb with a dustbin full of extra aubergine.

'Enjoy!' sniggered a voice from around the dining-room door.

Asti had come to gloat.

'I had pork steaks! So did Dad.'

Nelly's toes curled slightly, but she resisted the temptation to hurl the moussaka at the door. Instead, she removed the lid of the oven dish slowly and raised a serving spoon from the table.

'I can do this,' she whispered to herself, 'I can do this.'

Disappointed by the lack of niggle from her sister, Asti went up to her bedroom to pluck her eyebrows.

Nelly lowered the serving spoon into the dish and pressed it through the incinerated vegetable crust. The patchwork of charred aubergine slices folded under the pressure of the spoon, revealing an oil strike of tomato juice and curdled cream below.

There was a sludging rasp as Nelly lifted the spoon, like the sound of someone removing a Wellington from a bog.

'Think positive,' she told herself, 'think positive.'

As the spoon lifted from the oven dish, a twenty-five-tier tower of sloppy aubergine slices loomed into view. Slithery, pale, listless and lifeless, they clung to the spoon like of pile of old mould.

Nelly plopped the contents of the spoon on to her plate and swooned as a nostril full of vitamin A rose like a toad fart from her plate.

The blackened crust of the moussaka held firm on impact, but the lower twenty-four tiers slid unappetisingly in all directions. Nelly gritted her teeth and picked up her fork.

'I'm reaching *forward* and *placing* my fork into the first slice *there*,' she murmured. 'I'm reaching *forward* and *placing* my fork into the first slice *there*. I'M REACHING *FORWARD* . . .'

Nelly reached forward.

'AND *PLACING* MY FORK . . .'

Nelly stuck in her fork.

'INTO THE FIRST . . .'

Nelly wavered.

'SLICE *THERE* . . .'

With her eyes shut tight and her throat in traction, Nelly raised the forkful of moussaka to her lips. It slid into her mouth like a shovelful of grass cuttings, steamed by a summer sun into compost. Moist, warm and slimier than a slug's innards, the forkful of moussaka slithered its way to the back of her throat.

With a superhuman effort, Nelly summoned the willpower to swallow.

It didn't want to go down. The forkful of

moussaka wriggled in her throat like a wichetty grub, defying gravity with every squirm.

Finally, mercifully, it continued on its way.

Nelly gripped her throat and then hurled her fork across the table like a poker player discarding a losing hand.

'What's wrong with it?' glowered her mum, who had entered the dining room at precisely the wrong time.

'Nothing!' said Nelly. 'It's lovely, only I've already eaten . . . at the Altigators',' she fibbed.

'Well, why didn't you say?' said her mum, picking up the oven dish for reheating the following day.

'I forgot,' said Nelly. 'Sorry.'

Sorry? SORRY? She'd never been so relieved to escape from a kitchen table in her life.

That night, with her tummy gurgling, she picked up her school clothes and folded them away for the weekend. As she placed her jumper on to the highest shelf of her wardrobe her thoughts returned to the Altigators.

She walked into her mum and dad's bedroom and pressed her cheek flat to the far-right bedroom window. She could just about make out the silhouette of Éclair Towers, rising above the skyline in the distance.

Today's had been an eventful visit. But there was more monster-sitting work for her still to do.

'Stage three tomorrow!' she murmured. 'Positive petrol permitting!'

10

Four-star unleaded petrol, or rather the price of it, was the topic of conversation on the way over to the Towers the next day. Nelly's dad had got out of the wrong side of the bed that morning and had a bee in his bonnet about all the ferrying to and fro he and Mum had been doing for her lately.

'I'm all for you monster sitting, Nelly,' he said. 'You know Mum and I don't have a problem with that, but petrol isn't cheap, you know, what with it running out and the ozone layer and the North Sea.'

Nelly sat in her seat and kept schtum. When her dad was blowing a gasket it was always the best policy to let him huff and puff till he finally blew himself out.

'I mean, if I asked you to tell me the price of petrol per litre, could you? No, of course you couldn't. Petrol prices aren't your problem, are they? Oh no, when it comes to petrol prices leave it to Mum and Dad, they'll pay, they'll ferry me halfway across the world and back and keep filling up along the way. Never mind petrol prices.'

Nelly waited for the final puff.

'Or oil prices!' whistled her dad. 'A car doesn't run on petrol alone, oh no, there's dipsticks to think about too. What do you know about dipsticks? You wouldn't know a dipstick if it jumped out and hit you on the head. Go on, tell me where in this car you'd find a dipstick.'

Nelly looked at her dad and smiled sweetly.

'Didn't think so,' said Nelly's dad, tooting his horn at some jaywalking Saturday shoppers.

Nelly took some tissues from the glove compartment and then sat quietly as the car left the high street, circled the roundabout and turned into Éclair Way.

'What time do you want picking up?' said her

dad as they pulled up into the residents-only zone.

'One o'clock, please!' she said, leaning across to plant a kiss on her dad's cheek.

'I'm not having that leftover moussaka for tea,' grumbled her dad. 'I don't care how long it took Mum to make it.'

Nelly laughed. So that was why he was in such a bad mood.

She climbed out of the car and looked up at the Towers. She was becoming such a regular visitor, it was beginning to feel like her second home.

'One it is,' said her dad, moving the gear stick into reverse.

'Thanks, Dad,' smiled Nelly.

She closed the door of the car and turned in time to see the entrance door to the flats open. Her friends had seen her arrive. Hayley was first to emerge from the entrance, followed by an assortment of children. Unusually, Connor seemed to be hanging back.

He emerged from the building at the back of

the crowd, with his hands in his pockets and his head hung low.

'All right!' shouted Nelly, walking across the car park to meet them.

Hayley raised her hand and threaded her way between an old, yellow Datsun and a battered, green Fiesta.

'Hiya, Nelly!' she shouted. 'How you doin'?'

Nelly liked Hayley. In fact, she admired Hayley. For all the graffiti and trouble and gloom that surrounded the place she lived in, she always managed to stay cheerful.

'I'm good, thanks!' said Nelly, joining the children in the vacant parking space to the left of the burnt-out Orion. 'All right, Con?' she said, threading her eyes to the back of the crowd.

Connor kept his head low, and responded with a grunt and a shrug.

'Show her, Con,' said Hayley.

Nelly frowned as Connor lifted his head slowly. His eye was purple and swollen and his lip was split and grazed.

'Who did that to you?' gasped Nelly.

'Nutta,' said Hayley. 'Nutta punched him while the others held him down.'

'But why?' protested Nelly.

'His mobile phone,' explained Hayley. 'They've nicked his mobile phone.'

'But haven't you told your mum and dad, Con?' pressed Nelly.

'I haven't got a dad,' mumbled Connor.

'But what did your mum say? Mine would have gone mad!'

Hayley moved through the huddle of kids and put her arm around Connor's shoulders.

'Syko told Connor that if he said anything, they would torch his mum's car.'

'We can't afford another one,' mumbled Connor.

Nelly's toes curled inside her trainers. She was a centigrade away from boiling mad.

'But what about the police?' she said. 'Why don't you tell the police? After all, you know exactly where Nutta and Syko live. The police could get your phone back for you.'

'The police won't come here,' said Hayley, 'they're too scared.'

'That was a police car once,' said a small girl, pointing across the car park to the burnt-out shell of a patrol car, crunched into a distant line of broken concrete bollards.

'This is a no-go zone for the police,' said Hayley.

Nelly looked into Connor's blackened eye and then stared at the stern concrete face of the flats.

Boy, am I glad I don't live here, she thought.

Her watch said twelve but her heart said stay. If she hung around in the car park maybe she could confront Syko and Nutta herself. But the bullies and their gang were nowhere to be seen. Maybe they were skulking on the stairwell, maybe they were in town, shopping for fresh spray paint.

Nelly looked up at the top floor of the Towers. She had Altigators to visit.

'I have to go,' she said, smiling at Connor. 'I'm sure the swelling will soon go down, Con,' she said, 'and don't worry, if I see Nutta or Syko I'll get your mobile back.'

Connor smiled. They were nice words to hear. But he knew there was nothing Nelly could do.

Nelly thought differently. As she pushed the entrance door open, she was bristling for a confrontation with Nutta and Syko. She despised bullying and hated to see her friends on the receiving end of it.

But the entrance hall was bovver-boot free. There was no sign of the gang at ground level, and no grunts or echoing from the stairwell. Which was just as well. For the lift was out of action again.

Nelly lowered her finger from the button and dropped her shoulders. 'Twenty-five floors, here I come,' she sighed.

When she reached the top floor, she found Soar waiting for her at the very top of the stairs and Rise painting the walls of the hallway behind him.

'It's going to need another coat,' she cooed to Summit, who was cradled in the crook of the one arm that wasn't occupied with a paint roller.

'Hooligans have been writing on our walls

again, Nelly,' snapped Soar, waiting for her to reach the very top step so that he wouldn't have to look down. 'I don't know why they do it.'

Nelly stepped across the parquet floor and stared at the swathe of magnolia emulsion that Rise had just applied with the roller.

The faint pink outline of the oil-based graffiti paint had already begun to bleed through.

The words WEERDOS LIVE HERE had been sprayed large across the wall of the Altigators' flat.

'It makes the walls look so ugly, Nelly. We just don't understand what it's for, do we, Soar?' snipped Rise, tenderly rocking Summit with her free arm.

As Summit gurgled, Nelly shuddered. Éclair Towers was becoming her least favourite place in the world to be.

'I'm going to give Summit his lunch,' said Rise, 'and then I'll give the wall another coat when it's dry. Would you like me to make you a sandwich, Nelly? I've got some Dairylea triangles in the fridge.'

Nelly smiled and shook her head. Dairylea triangles? That was the last thing she expected Altigators to eat.

Rise stepped into the flat to the customary sound of heavy-metal rock music and closed the door behind her. The moment she was inside, Summit began to scream.

'Nelly,' snapped Soar, from the top of the stairs, 'in all my life, I've never asked anyone to do something for me, but I need you to help me do this.'

Nelly turned back to the stairwell to find Soar pumped up and ready to go. His large orange eye was blazing with frustration and the scales of his muscular white arms were flexed to sinew-breaking point.

'You have to help me conquer my fear of depths, Nelly,' he snapped.

Nelly walked to the top of the stairwell and slipped Soar's huge bony claws into her hand.

'You really want this badly, don't you, Soar?' she whispered.

'Real bad,' he snapped.

'Then let's do it!' she smiled.

Soar and Nelly turned to face the stairwell. 'OK,' said Nelly. 'Remember everything I said to you yesterday. Close your eyes – sorry, I mean eye – and let the positive petrol fill your veins!'

Soar's huge, hairy eyelid slid shut and the toes of his platform shoes inched closer to the edge of the stairs.

'We're stepping *forward* . . .' coaxed Nelly.

'AND *PLACING* OUR FEET *ON THE VERY TOP* OF THE NEXT STEP *THERE*!' chanted Soar, lowering his jaws a fraction towards the stairs.

'Good,' said Nelly. 'Now this time we go for it, OK? Soar, this time it's for real.'

Soar's claws tightened around Nelly's fingers and the toes of his platform shoes readjusted.

'One, two, three . . .' said Nelly. 'WE'RE STEPPING *FORWARD* AND *PLACING* OUR FEET *ON THE VERY TOP* OF THE NEXT STEP *THERE*!'

With a tug and a squeeze, Nelly and Soar stepped down on to the first step.

Soar opened his eye. 'Have we done it?' he snapped, too nervous to look down.

Nelly squeezed his hand. '*You've* done it, Soar,' she beamed. 'That wasn't so hard, was it?'

'Time for lunch,' said Soar, turning towards the flat door.

'No, no, no!' exclaimed Nelly. 'Not so fast. We haven't quite accomplished stage three yet.'

Soar pointed his jaws at the ceiling. 'We can finish stage three tomorrow,' he snapped.

'No,' said Nelly firmly. 'We're going to complete stage three RIGHT NOW!'

The air-balloon tattoo on Soar's left shoulder deflated slightly as his body slumped at the prospect.

'Come on, Soar,' coaxed Nelly, 'you can do it. Be positive and you can do it.'

'YOUR SANDWICH IS READY!' snapped Rise, opening the door to the flat and filling the hallway with a crescendo of rock music and baby screams.

'I can do it, I CAN do it,' murmured Soar, gripping Nelly's fingers like a vice.

Nelly decided to let her fingers suffer in silence rather than break Soar's concentration and resolve.

'I'M STEPPING, *FORWARD* . . .'

Soar inched his toe towards the lip of the step.

'AND *PLACING* MY FOOT . . .'

Soar lifted his foot from the step.

'PLACING MY FOOT . . . PLACING MY FOOT . . .'

His foot froze in mid-air.

'On the *very top* . . .' coaxed Nelly gently.

Soar responded to the squeeze of his hand and nervously began to feel for the next step with his toe.

'OF THE NEXT . . . *STEP THERE*!'

The sole of Soar's shoe touched down like a spaceship and his furry eyelid flew open.

'I've done it!' he snapped, drawing his other foot confidently down on to the same level. 'Two steps! Look, Rise, TWO WHOLE STEPS! I can do it!'

Rise crept to the top of the stairs, with Summit in one arm and a plate of sandwiches in the other.

'I'll take your word for it,' she snapped, unable to bring herself to look down.

'Are you ready for stage four, Soar? Are you ready for stage four?' cheered Nelly.

'Absolutely not!' snapped Soar, stepping back up on to the landing and grabbing a sandwich from the plate. 'You can't rush these things, Nelly,' he said, snapping his jaws through the circular cardboard box of Dairylea triangles that Rise had sandwiched between a large bread bap.

Nelly sighed and trudged to the top of the stairs. At this rate she would be an old woman before Soar had descended the stairs to ground level.

'How many stages are there *D-word* to floor twenty-four?' asked Soar with a munch.

Nelly counted in her head. 'There are two flights of ten steps. That's twenty stages,' she surmised. 'So there are five hundred steps down to ground level.'

Soar paused in mid-chew. That was a lot of positive petrol.

'Of course, you could always take the lift,' said Nelly.

'You know what I think about lifts,' snapped Soar. '*Lifts* indeed!' he growled. '*Sinks*, more like.'

Nelly decided her work was done for the day and resisted the Altigators' invitation to enter the heavy-metal screech of the flat. She wasn't sure her ears could take the decibels, but also, if she left the Altigators now, she would have time to catch up with Hayley and Connor before she returned home.

With a wave and a double thumbs-up, she vanished down the stairs.

11

All was not well when she stepped out through the door of the ground-floor entrance hall. Despite the sunny disposition of the weather, a group of adults were squaring up to each other in the car park, with faces as black as thunder.

Fingers were jabbing, fists were flying and handbags were swinging.

Nelly drew her back against the wall of the tower and then skirted in a wide arc away from the trouble. As she slipped behind the screen of a high wall, she found Hayley, Connor and their friends perched on six wheelie-bins, peeking at the kerfuffle.

'Help me up,' said Nelly, holding up her hands.

Connor jumped. He had been so engrossed in the argument that he hadn't noticed Nelly approaching.

'Don't do that!' he said, turning his blackened eye round to Nelly. 'I thought you were Nutta!'

Nelly apologised and then pressed the soles of her trainers against the sheer face of a bin, as Connor hauled her up. 'What's going on?' she whispered, kneeling down on the warm, rubber lid.

'They're arguing about that car,' whispered Connor. 'We think Nutta's dad has sold that bloke that car, but the bloke has brought it back 'cos there's something wrong with it.'

Nelly peeped over the wall. 'What bloke? What car?' she whispered. It was difficult to separate anyone from the tangle of fists and handbags.

Connor hooked his finger over the wall and pointed to a large-bellied man in a white T-shirt, who was throwing haymaker punches in all directions.

'He's the one who bought the car,' whispered Connor, 'and that's Nutta's dad in the tattoos.'

'In the tattoos' just about summed Nutta's dad up, for apart from a pair of brown trousers belted around his middle, he appeared to wearing nothing but blue ink. From the waist up, tattoos emblazoned every inch of his body, barbed wire scarred his knuckles, serpents writhed up his forearms, dragons fought on his shoulders, eagles swooped from his chest and the fires of hell leapt from his neck. Across both of his unshaven cheeks spiders' webs stretched like trapeze nets and across his forehead were the four letters H-A-T-E.

Nelly stared in disbelief. There was enough ink on Nutta's dad to fill three exercise books. And there was enough width on his forehead to write CONSTANTINOPLE.

'Which one is Syko's dad?' whispered Nelly, wincing as Granny Nutta launched into the big-bellied T-shirt with a swipe of her handbag.

'Syko's dad's on the floor, wrestling with the other bloke,' said Hayley.

Nelly bobbed her head up just far enough to see a second flurry of fists and feet erupting at exhaust-pipe level. Two large men were trying to wheel-clamp each other with headlocks. The white Volkswagen Beetle that they were arguing about shook as the two men crunched into the driver's door, and then the front of the car crumpled as they lurched to their feet and toppled headlong over the bonnet and on to the ground. Syko's dad was first to his feet. He shook his head like a horse and then directed a broken-toothed yell at his opponent.

Syko's dad was wiry like his son, although hours of working out with weights had transformed his wiry bits into steel cables. His arms bulged like stockings full of coconuts and the veins in his neck rippled like steel cable. With a scream like a baboon, he dragged his opponent on to the bonnet and launched into a volley of punches again.

'Does this happen very often?' whispered Nelly.

'About two or three times a week,' replied Hayley.

'They love fighting,' whispered Connor. 'Both families love fighting.'

The arrival of two more handbags confirmed

'Does this happen very often?'

as much. Nutta and Syko's mothers had suddenly returned from shopping in town and had now lent their own fury to the fray.

'They've got tattoos too!' gasped Nelly, trying to work out whether the matching tattoos emblazoned across the bridges of the women's noses were hamsters or something more sinister.

'They're black rats,' whispered Hayley. 'The tails of the tattoos are curled around one eye.'

'I thought they were wearing monocles!' whispered Nelly.

She bobbed her head down and watched with the other children as the warring adults tumbled across the white Beetle like a gang of panel beaters. By the time the fight broke up it was difficult to tell which looked worse, the adults or the car. With a volley of angry shouts and some not-very-nice hand gestures, Syko and Nutta's dads sent the visitors packing from the car park.

'Now you can see why we don't mess with them,' whispered Hayley.

Nelly took a deep breath. This was worse than

watching the six o'clock news. She felt sick to the pit of her stomach that her friends should have to live with trouble like this.

She felt even worse when she turned to climb down from the bin.

'That'll be two pounds each, please,' said Nutta, puffing a ring of cigar smoke up at the bins.

'Three pounds for you, Sardine,' grinned Syko, ' 'cos you don't live here.'

All of the children froze as they looked down to see the rest of the gang, circling the bins.

'I don't think so,' said Nelly defiantly.

'Oh, I DO think so,' said Syko, lashing out at the bin with his boot. 'You see, our families have just put on a little show and you scumbags have just helped yourselves to the best seats in the house.'

'Without paying,' puffed Nutta.

'Yeah, wivvout payin',' bleated the rest of the gang.

'So pay up,' growled Syko.

Nelly fixed Syko's stare with a steely glare of

her own. 'You're not getting anything from me. But I'll have something from you. Give Connor back his phone NOW.'

Connor shifted uncomfortably on his bin lid. 'It's all right, Nelly,' he whispered.

Nelly shook her head. 'It's not all right, Con. The phone doesn't belong to them, it belongs to you. Now give it BACK!' she glared.

Nutta placed the cigar into his mouth and drew long and hard. It wasn't often that someone showed the courage to stand up to him and Syko, and he wanted to milk it for as long as he could.

'Aaah, Sardine,' he sneered through a cloud of stinking tobacco smoke. 'I think we may have a bit of a problem here, because I'm sorry to say that I have given the phone that I FOUND yesterday to MY DAD. Perhaps you would care to knock on the door of our flat and ask for it back.'

Nelly stared down at the ground. Perhaps she wouldn't.

'Flat 24A is the address you'll be wanting,' sneered Nutta.

Nelly turned and looked over the wall of the car park. The fight had dispersed now and there was no one around to prevent an escape in that direction. The only problem was, it was a three-metre drop down to the ground.

'Pay up NOW,' growled Syko, holding out a nicotine-fingered palm.

'Get lost,' said Nelly, deciding to adopt the mediaeval-castle strategy of defending from higher ground.

Syko and Nutta turned to each other with Rottweiler smiles. 'Get 'em, lads,' they ordered.

The bovver-booted legs of the gang strode forward and a volley of knuckles arrowed themselves to the handles of the bins.

'I do believe these bins are full,' laughed Nutta.

'Then it is our civic duty to empty them,' grunted Syko.

One by one, the gang members turned their backs to the bins and began straining to pull them away. With their arms at full stretch and their grunts at full grunt, the gang lay siege to the wheelie-bin castles. Nelly and her friends gripped their lids with both hands in a desperate attempt to keep their balance. But as each bin tipped forward it became impossible to stay on.

The smaller children fell from their turrets first, followed by Hayley and then Connor. Nelly refused to give in. She gripped the sides of her bin-lid like a girl possessed and spread her knees wider in an attempt to stay on. Each time another pair of hands attached to the handle of her bin she despatched it with a thump of her fist.

'Get off!' she shouted. 'Get lost!' she cried. 'DAD!' she cheered. 'DAD! I'm over here!'

Everyone stared over their shoulders. Nelly's dad was sitting in the car park staring at the wall, trying to work out how Nelly had mysteriously doubled in height. He had seen her head and shoulders surfing up and down behind the wall, but it had never occurred to him that she might have been in trouble. He acknowledged her shouts with a cheery wave.

At the mention of the word 'Dad', Syko, Nutta and the gang immediately melted away.

'We'll getchoo, Sardine!' they shouted from the safe distance of the bottle bank.

Nelly jumped down from her wheelie bin and dusted herself down.

As brave as she was and as angry as she felt, another confrontation with Syko and Nutta was the last thing that she wanted.

12

There became a cat and mouse element to Nelly's ensuing visits to Éclair Towers. Just like Hayley and Connor, she found herself entering the flats and climbing the stairwell with caution. On the occasions that she caught a glimpse of Syko and Nutta, she either quickened her step or slipped quietly out of sight until they had passed. Cowardly it might sound. But smart thinking it most certainly was.

Although the lift had remained broken and her calf muscles had doubled in size, her visits to Flat 25A had become a towering success. After one week, Soar had managed to descend a full six steps of the stairwell all by himself and by the end of week two he had walked to the bottom of the first flight with his eyes open.

'I don't know how I'll ever thank you for this,' he snapped, as they walked ten steps back up on to the landing.

'You can start with a Dairylea sandwich,' laughed Nelly.

Rise met them in the hallway and beckoned them inside the flat.

'Have you been painting your walls again?' said Nelly, picking up on the distinctive smell of fresh paint.

'The people with the spray cans came back yesterday evening,' sighed Rise.

'Why do they do it?' snapped Soar.

'Because they're dipsticks,' said Nelly.

She followed Soar and Rise to the door of the flat and then covered her ears as Rise pulled it open. The heavy-metal music inside the flat was so loud that even the floorboards were shaking.

'I THINK SUMMIT'S WOKEN UP AGAIN!' sighed Rise, hurrying across to the cot in her high heels.

I'm going to have to ask these Altigators,

thought Nelly, why on earth do they play their music so loud?

'CAN YOU GET ME A DUMMY, SOAR?' cried Rise. 'SUMMIT WON'T SUCK MY CLAWS, THEY STILL TASTE OF TURPS!'

As Soar scuttled off in the direction of the dummy drawer, Nelly drifted across to the window with her Dairylea sandwich.

The view from the flat was majestic. She could see right across the grey-slated rooftops of the Montelimar Estate as far as Paramount Hill. In the distance, to the west, she could see the golf course spreading like billiard baize across the Downs and on the furthermost reaches of the Estate, the industrial estate paraded its grid system like a little piece of Manhattan.

'WHAT A VIEW, SOAR!' exclaimed Nelly as the Altigator joined her by the window. 'YOU CAN PRACTICALLY SEE THE WHOLE OF LOWBRIDGE FROM HERE!'

Soar shifted a little uncomfortably on his platform heels.

'CAN YOU?' he snapped. 'I WOULDN'T KNOW, I'VE NEVER LOOKED DOWN.'

Nelly rocked on her heels. 'SOAR? YOU'VE *NEVER* LOOKED DOWN?' she gasped. 'YOU LIVE IN THE TOP FLAT OF ÉCLAIR TOWERS WITH THIS WONDERFUL VIEW AND YOU'VE *NEVER LOOKED DOWN*?'

'WE ALWAYS LOOK *UP* AT THE CLOUDS,' Soar coughed.

Nelly had heard everything now. She placed her hands on her hips and then stepped directly in front of Soar, with her back against the window.

'LOOK AT ME, SOAR. LOOK *D-WORD* INTO MY EYES RIGHT NOW!'

Soar's furry eyelid blinked upwards at the ceiling for a moment and then slowly he lowered his jaws.

'NOW THEN,' shouted Nelly above the floor-rattling music, 'KEEP LOOKING ME IN THE EYES, SOAR, BECAUSE ON THE COUNT OF FIVE I'M GOING TO STEP TO ONE SIDE. AND WHEN I DO STEP AWAY I WANT YOU TO KEEP LOOKING *D-WORD*. OK?'

Soar nodded his head nervously.

Nelly began her count to five, but on the count of three she deviously jumped to one side. Before Soar had had even half a chance to close his eyes he found himself staring down at an aerial view of Lowbridge.

'IT'S AMAZING!' he gasped. 'IT'S INCREDIBLE. WHAT'S THAT BUILDING DOWN THERE?' he said, pointing to the south.

'THAT'S LOWBRIDGE CITY FOOTBALL GROUND,' shouted Nelly.

'AND WHAT'S THAT PLACE RIGHT OVER THERE?' he snapped.

'THAT'S WHERE ASTI WILL BE TAKEN ONE DAY,' smiled Nelly, looking at the mental hospital.

'AND DOWN THERE?'

'A CHURCH.'

'AND OVER THERE?'

'OVER THERE IS WHERE I LIVE!' laughed Nelly.

Soar stepped closer to the window and then pointed his jaws directly down.

'AND WHAT'S THAT DOWN THERE?' he snapped.

'THAT'S THE CAR PARK,' shouted Nelly. 'AND THOSE ARE THE WHEELIE BINS AND THAT'S THE BOTTLE BANK.'

Soar pressed the top of his head to the window pane and radared the ground below in all directions.

'DO YOU KNOW WHAT, NELLY?' he snapped. 'I THINK TOMORROW I WILL BE READY FOR STAGE TWENTY!'

Nelly slapped an affectionate arm around the rock-hard muscular contours of the Altigator's waist.

'DO YOU KNOW WHAT, SOAR?' she laughed. 'I DO BELIEVE YOU ARE RIGHT!'

13

When Nelly arrived at Éclair Towers the next afternoon, there were two surprises waiting for her. At long last someone had picked up that fish and chip wrapper by the main entrance door, and, miracle of miracles, the lift was working again.

Nelly stabbed the button of Floor 25 with her finger and turned to read the lift walls. A few graffitied bulletins had been added since her last journey – *Man U* now ruled *OK, Phil woz ere, Shaz* was a *bleep bleep bleep,* and *Nutta* had promoted himself to *God.*

As the lift approached the top floor, Nelly turned to face the four screw fixings where the mirror should have been and smoothed her sweatshirt. The lift rocked as the mechanism came to a halt and the doors slid open with a rattle.

'Nelly! So good to see you!' snip-snapped Soar, who was waiting for her outside with open arms. 'It only seems like yesterday!' he joked.

'And the day before that, and the day before that, and the day before that, and the day before that . . . !' laughed Nelly. 'Are you ready for the big day, Soar?' she asked.

'Ready as I'll ever be!' he snapped.

Nelly stepped out of the lift into the hallway and was greeted by Rise and a furious bundle of blankets.

'He's been crying all morning,' snapped Soar.

'He needs his sleep,' snipped Rise.

Nelly peered into the blankets. The more that Rise rocked Summit, the more he seemed to scream.

'Oh dear,' said Nelly, giving Summit a gentle rasp on the cheek with her finger. 'Perhaps he's teething?'

'Far too young for that, Nelly,' snipped Rise with a shake of her jaws. 'Please do come inside.'

Nelly winced as she stepped through the door into the Altigators' flat. The heavy-metal music that filled the room was now so loud that the vibrations were beginning to loosen the nails from the floorboards.

'TAKE A SEAT!' shouted Soar, pointing to the stools.

'THANKS!' hollered Nelly.

She walked to the stools, but as she reached out to grab one, the vibrations in the room sent them juddering across the floor.

'I THINK I'LL STAND!' she shouted, bending down to pull up her socks.

Her ankles were shaking, her body was humming and her brain cells were jiggling like blended coffee beans.

Soar lumbered towards Rise and prodded Summit's blankets tenderly with his claw.

Summit responded with a wail.

'HE'S NOT HAPPY,' shouted Soar, a picture of misery himself. 'HE'S NOT HAPPY AT ALL.'

Nelly walked towards the cot, but as she

reached out her hands to comfort Summit, Rise and Soar, her attention was drawn to the wall by a clatter. At the far end of the room the high-heeled shoe display was avalanching from the shelves.

Even worse, the vibrations of the music had begun to shake the porcelain bird collection from its high-level roost. One by one, the china birds dropped like fledglings from their roosts and shattered into pieces on the floor.

Rise put her head in her hands and began to wail too.

Soar raised his jaws to the ceiling and his eye began to glaze.

'SOAR!' shouted Nelly, determined to rescue the situation.

'Yes, Nelly?' murmured Soar.

'HAVE YOU EVER THOUGHT OF TURNING THE MUSIC DOWN?' she hollered.

'MANY TIMES,' shouted Soar.

'OR EVEN BETTER, OFF?' shouted Nelly.

'MANY TIMES,' shouted Soar.

'THEN DO IT!' screamed Nelly.

Soar lowered his jaws and fixed Nelly with a stare so intense it could have curdled cement. The claws on both hands tightened into granite balls and the biceps in his arms bulged.

'I *WILL* DO IT,' he snapped. 'I WILL DO TURN THE MUSIC OFF *RIGHT NOW*!'

With a velociraptor roar, Soar turned in his platform shoes and marched towards the front door of the flat. Nelly chased after him, totally confused.

'Wait here, Nelly,' roared Soar from the top of the stairwell. 'I have some business to attend to.'

And with that, he stomped out of sight down the stairs.

Nelly raced back to the flat and then covered her ears as a familiar voice exploded through the floorboards from the flat below.

'WILL YOU TURN YOUR MUSIC DOWN! WE'RE TRYING TO GET A BABY TO SLEEP UP HERE!'

The sound of spintering wood was suddenly

followed by abrupt silence as a music system was ripped from its sockets.

Nelly ran to the window of the flat and looked down, just in time to see a Sony Separates CD-system smash through the plate-glass window and plummet twenty-four floors on to the recycling bins.

Soar had snapped, big time, in the flat directly below.

What happened next can only be described as *World War Three Meets Godzilla × Ten*. There were bangs, there were crashes, there were shouts and there were screeches. There were clatters and screams, hollers and wails – but after an assortment of furniture had howitzered out of the window . . .

. . . there was silence.

Wonderful, peaceful, silence.

'AND GET SOME FRESH PAINT ON THOSE WALLS!' roared Soar, shattering the peace momentarily with one parting volley. 'THEY'RE AN ABSOLUTE DISGRACE!'

Soar returned from Flat 24A with his orange

eye still blazing and his chest still pumping.

'I've been wanting to do that for years!' he said, composing himself with a couple of long, deep breaths. 'Thank you Nelly, I could never have done it without you.'

Nelly's mouth opened, but it required a couple of practise gulps before she could speak.

'Did you throw their stereo out of the window, Soar?' she asked.

'Yes I did,' snapped Soar. 'It's been plaguing us ever since we moved here. I've threatened to throw the whole family out of the window if I hear their music again.'

'What did they say?'

'The man came at me with a chair leg and the women tried to whack me with their handbags.'

'Handbags?' gasped Nelly. 'Was the man covered in tattoos?'

'That's right,' snapped Soar. 'Really sissy ones.'

Nelly gasped. Soar had single-handedly sorted out the Nuttas!

'Summit is asleep!' beamed Rise.

The news just got better and better.

Nelly stayed to help sweep up the broken porcelain and return the high-heeled shoes to their display shelves.

'You will let me come back and monster sit for you, won't you, Soar?' she asked.

'Of course we will, Nelly,' smiled Soar. 'We can't eat all that cheese spread by ourselves!'

Nelly blew a kiss into Summit's cot and then shook Soar and Rise by the hand.

'I'll wave up to you from the car park,' Nelly smiled.

'I'll be sure to be looking down,' laughed Soar.

'I'll wave from the stools,' shuddered Rise.

Both Altigators followed Nelly to the lift and waited with her for the doors to slide open.

'Are you sure you don't want to try the lift, Soar?' said Nelly. 'It really is the easiest way to travel!'

'No thank you, Nelly,' shuddered Soar. 'I shall be sticking to the stairs!'

Nelly stepped into the lift and pushed the ground-floor button.

'Going *D-word*!' she laughed.

The lift doors closed with a clunk and a rattle and Soar and Rise's waving claws finally disappeared from view.

Nelly sighed contentedly. She had invested so much time and energy in the Altigators, it was so good to see all her hard work pay off.

She leant back against the wall of the lift and began the countdown to ground level.

Floor fifteen, floor fourteen, floor thirteen, floor twelve, eleven, ten, nine, nine, nine . . . the lift had stopped at floor nine!

Nelly stepped forward to push the button to continue down, but as she did so the lift doors slid open.

She had company. Grunting, swearing, cigar-puffing company.

'Well, well, well,' puffed Nutta, stepping into the lift. 'If it isn't our old friend, Sardine!'

'Long time no see, Sardine!' belched Syko, lobbing an empty lager can on to the floor of the lift.

Nelly stepped back as Nutta, Syko and four of their cronies forced their way into the lift before the doors closed.

'Nowhere, please,' grinned Syko, pushing the hold button on the lift.

Nelly closed her eyes and turned away as Nutta leant close to her and blew a cloud of cigar smoke confidently into her face. Word of his parents' downfall obviously hadn't reached him.

'I do believe we have an old argument to settle, Sardine,' he leered.

'Three pounds I think it is you owe us,' growled Syko.

'Plus interest,' leered Nutta.

'That makes it *five* pounds you owe us,' sneered Syko.

Nelly opened her eyes and stared at both gang leaders in turn.

'I haven't got any money on me,' she said, 'and if I did have, you wouldn't get any of it, anyway.'

Syko looked at Nutta and grinned.

'Oh dear. Sardine can't pay up. That means it's PUNISHMENT TIME!'

Nutta and the other four cronies began cracking their knuckles as Syko assumed the role of executioner.

'Now then,' he leered, 'what's the best way to punish a sardine . . . ? Um . . . let me think. Ahh . . . of course. Squash them! Sardines love to be squashed inside a tin, don't you!'

Nelly gasped as the six thugs shoulder-charged her into the metal lift wall and then pressed her like soft Blu-tak into the lift panel.

'SQUEEEEEEZZZZE!' laughed Nutta, as Nelly tried her best to push them off with her forearms and elbows.

'SQQQQUUUEEEEEEEEEEEE—EEK!' squawked Syko, as the service panel in the roof above them suddenly clattered down on to their heads and the giant emerald jaws of an Altigator thrust themselves through the hole.

All six thugs dropped to their knees and cowered on the floor.

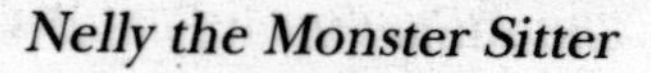

***'WHAT'S GOING ON IN HERE,'* he roared.**

'WHAT'S GOING ON IN HERE?' roared Soar, steaming the air above their heads with his nostrils.

'WHO'S BEEN SMOKING CIGARS?' he roared.

'He has,' squealed Syko, pointing at Nutta.

'WHO'S BEEN DRINKING BEER?' he snapped.

'He has,' squealed Nutta, pointing at Syko.

'YOU'RE FAR TOO YOUNG TO BE DRINKING AND SMOKING!' roared Soar.

'We won't do it again,' squeaked Nutta and Syko.

Soar turned his big, hairy eyelid towards Nelly and winked.

'AND WHO'S BEEN GRAFFITIING ALL THIS FILTHY RUBBISH ALL OVER THESE WALLS?' roared Soar.

'They have!' squealed Nutta and Syko, pointing trembling fingers at their four accomplices.

'YOU'VE GOT TWENTY-FOUR HOURS TO CLEAN IT UP, DO YOU UNDERSTAND ME?' roared Soar.

The four cronies placed their hands over their heads and curled up into spineless hedgehogs.

Nelly winked back at Soar, reached across and released the hold button on the lift.

'Going down,' she smiled.

As the lift restarted its journey through the floors below, Soar reached down with his boulder-strength arms and lifted Nutta and Syko clean off the floor. As he drew them bleating towards the lift hatch, he paused to study the width of Nutta's forehead.

'If I'm not mistaken,' he hissed, drawing Nutta's nose stud a centimetre from his flaring nostrils, 'I've already acquainted myself with YOUR family.'

Nutta closed his eyes and began to squeak like a mouse.

'But *YOU*,' Soar snapped, drawing Syko to his jaws like a toothpick, 'I DON'T BELIEVE I'VE HAD THE PLEASURE OF MEETING *YOUR* FAMILY. WHICH FLAT DO YOU LIVE IN?'

'9A,' squeaked Syko.

The lift reached the ground level with a bump.

'WELL, AFTER WE'VE SAID GOODBYE TO NELLY, I'M GOING TO PAY A VISIT TO 9A. I WANT TO HAVE A QUIET WORD WITH YOUR FATHER TOO!'

Syko nodded timidly, his bovver boots dangling like a rag doll.

The lift doors opened and Nelly stepped, grinning, into the entrance hall. She was followed by a cowering, squeaking, quaking collection of shaven heads and bovver boots.

The lift doors tried to close, but Soar parted them like curtains and strode powerfully into the hall.

'AND WHO'S RESPONSIBLE FOR THIS?' he roared, scanning the graffitied walls of the entrance hall and then turning disdainfully towards the staircase with a sniff.

'He is,' said every gang member, pointing at each other.

Soar brought his platformed heel stomping down on to the floor.

'WELL, CLEAN IT UP, YOU DIPSTICKS!' roared Soar. 'THIS IS ÉCLAIR TOWERS, NOT A PIGSTY!'

As the gang got ready to run, Soar hooked his claw under the collar of Syko's T-shirt.

'BEFORE YOU MINI-GANGSTERS DISAPPEAR,' he snapped, 'I WILL JUST SAY ONE MORE THING.'

No one was going to argue.

Soar lifted Syko by the collar and strode across the hall to stand alongside Nelly.

'THIS YOUNG LADY HERE,' he snapped, 'IS A VERY GOOD FRIEND OF MINE.'

Nelly looked up and smiled at him as he placed his free hand gently on her shoulder.

'AND IF I EVER FIND THAT ANY OF YOU HAVE SO MUCH AS BREATHED ON ONE HAIR OF HER HEAD . . .'

'Or any of my friends' heads,' added Nelly.

'. . . THEN I WILL SHAKE YOU LIKE SPRAY CANS UNTIL YOU RATTLE!' roared Soar. **'NOW CLEAR OFF!'**

As Nutta and the four cronies scarpered up the stairs, Nelly threw herself at Soar and gave him a hug.

'How did you know I was in trouble?' she asked.

Soar stroked her hair with the claws of his free hand. 'When you didn't appear in the car park I guessed you'd got stuck in the lift.'

'But you *HATE* lifts!' cried Nelly. 'You're *TERRIFIED* of lifts!'

'Sometimes you just have to conquer your fears,' smiled Soar.

'Now then,' he growled, dangling Syko in front of his jaws. 'This chap and I are going to pay a visit to Flat 9A.'

Syko closed his eyes with a squeak and began kicking out wildly with his boots.

'Going up!' roared Soar, pressing the button on the lift.

As the lift doors closed, Nelly made her way spiritedly through the entrance door and into the car park outside. She skipped to the burnt-out Orion and turned to look up at the Towers.

She was just in time to see the second stereo system of the day explode through a plate-glass window and another shower of music CDs bounce like hailstones on to the ground.

Éclair Towers was never the same from that day. The next time she saw Hayley and Connor, they were all smiles and mobile phones. The next time she saw Nutta and Syko's family, they were wearing overalls and repainting the walls. One Sunday she even saw them coming out of church! The burnt-out cars were removed from the car park, dish cloths were replaced by window boxes, the stairwell was transformed with the whiff of magnolia paint and the residents were even lucky enough to get a new caretaker.

It you ever go to Éclair Towers and you're in need of his assistance, take the lift to Flat 25A.